Mountain Light

Laurence Yep

H
A Division

To
Wing Tek Lum
who makes connections

Mountain Light
Copyright © 1985 by Laurence Yep
All rights reserved. No part of this book may be
used or reproduced in any manner whatsoever without
written permission except in the case of brief quotations
embodied in critical articles and reviews.
Printed in the United States of America.
For information address
HarperCollins Children's Books,
a division of HarperCollins Publishers,
10 East 53rd Street,
New York, NY 10022.

Library of Congress Cataloging-in-Publication Data
Yep, Laurence.
Mountain light.
Summary: Swept up in one of the local rebellions
against the Manchus in China, nineteen-year-old Squeaky
travels to America to seek his fortune among the gold
fields of California.
[1. China—History—19th century—Fiction.
2. Emigration and immigration—Fiction.] I. Title.
PZ7.Y44Mo 1985 [Fic] 85-42643
ISBN 0-06-440667-9 (pbk.)

First Harper Trophy edition, 1997.

Harper Trophy® is a registered trademark of
HarperCollins Publishers Inc.

Author's Note

When I first began writing DRAGONWINGS over twenty-five years ago, I also began creating stories about one family, the Youngs of Three Willows village, who had an ongoing love affair with America.

Most books of that time viewed the evolution of Chinese Americans from either the Chinese side or the American side; but I wanted to do both. Through the Young family, I tried to show how rebellions, wars, and famine in China forced many to make the dangerous voyage to America. As gold miners in California, the Youngs—like many others—used their wits to survive the lawless frontier (THE SERPENT'S CHILDREN and MOUNTAIN LIGHT).

The next generation of Youngs helped build the transcontinental railroad—risking death in many ways and living beneath the snow during the worst winter of the century (DRAGON'S GATE). And, for better or for worse, they realized that their future lay in America.

The Young family matured with the American West, sinking their roots deep into American thought and technology. In DRAGONWINGS, their development continued through their surrogate, Bright Star, their "classmate" from the railroad.

Subsequent generations of Youngs became so American that ironically some of their members, like Casey Young, lost track of the Chinese part of their identity and had to discover it again (CHILD OF THE OWL and THIEF OF HEARTS).

In their adventures over a century, the generations of the Young family represent my version of Chinese America—in all of its tears and its laughter.

CHIEN, the fifty-third
hexagram
from the
Book of Changes

Chapter One

I got ready with my knife when I heard the footsteps outside the house. If the Manchus were going to kill me, I'd try to take some of them with me; but knowing myself, that wasn't likely. I'd find some way to botch it. I'd lived my life like a clumsy clown, and I was going to die like one.

Smoke from the burning village drifted through the windows. When I had seen the corpses in the street and the houses burning, I had figured that the Manchus were up to their old tricks. Ever since they had conquered the Middle Kingdom two centuries ago, we'd been trying to get rid of them and they had kept coming back and killing. At any rate, I thought I would be safe enough for now because the Manchus had already swept through this village. But I'd been wrong—as usual, my uncle Itchy would have said.

He'd warned me that I'd been a fool to march off to fight against the Manchus. I could see his face, wrinkled like an old apricot, scowling at me. "Let other fools do the dying. That's what they're good for. You're one of the Laus of Phoenix Village. If you've got to fight anything, fight the beetles in our fields."

Not for the first time, I found myself wishing that I'd listened to him. Joining the Revolution had sounded so glorious. I'd swaggered off expecting to find a camp of heroes waving banners and instead had found a lot of dirty, flea-bitten bandits arguing with one another about who ought to get a bigger share of the loot. No wonder the Manchus had scattered us like a flock of geese.

The door creaked open, and in the rectangle of bright sunlight I saw three shadows stretch across the floor toward the wall. Even as I lunged, I noticed that one shadow was smaller than the others. I had one moment to see the faces of two men and a girl.

Both men had their hair done up in an antique topknot just like mine—even though the Manchus commanded us to wear a queue instead. The girl was wearing the red turban of a rebel. And they were all looking as desperate as me.

And then the girl was gone and I felt a foot clip my right leg out from under me while hands grasped my wrist and yanked me forward, and I was flying through the air straight toward the opposite wall. I managed to throw out one hand to cushion the impact, but my face still hit hard. I could feel the tears blurring my eyes and a saltiness on my lips as if my much-abused nose were bleeding.

Before I could even cry out in pain, a knee jammed the small of my back hard, driving the breath out of my lungs. Fingers again seized my knife hand and twisted it around behind my back. "Drop it," the girl said, "or I'll break this arm."

She spoke in the dialect of the Four Districts. I never thought that I'd hear it here in the Three Districts around Canton. In fact, there had been something familiar about her face. "All right," I said hurriedly and let go of the knife. She snatched it from me with her free hand. "I'm a friend, after all."

"Banish the Darkness," the man said.

I gave the rebel's countersign. "Restore the Light." The Darkness was the symbol for the Manchu dynasty.

But the girl seemed determined to find some excuse to do me bodily harm. "He might be a spy who has picked up the passwords."

And in my panic at that moment all I could think of was what my uncle would have said. "Don't you think the Manchus could hire better spies than me?"

"If he were a spy," the man suggested softly, as if he were coaxing the girl out of a tantrum, "we would have been dead by now."

"You've taught me enough so that I bet I could take on a real spy," the girl protested, but she let go of my hand and stood up.

I rolled over on my back and looked up at her. She was small and thin, with a high, flat forehead over narrow eyes and a long, slender nose. Now that I had a chance to study her face, I was sure that I'd seen her before. "I know you from somewhere."

She tucked my knife behind her back within her sash. "I think I've seen you before too." And she drew her eyebrows together intently.

"That's possible." I sat up and began to rub the wrist that she had twisted. "Have you ever been to Phoenix Village?" The next thing I knew, she had the knife out again and was touching the point against my neck. "Did I say something wrong?"

She nodded toward the scar on my cheek. "I thought I recognized that decoration."

I smiled nervously. She really looked ready to use that knife. "My cousin Lumpy put it there. We were playing swordfight with some sharp sticks. Actually, it was more his idea than mine to fight with sticks. He's something of a bully, and—"

She pressed the knife point ever so slightly deeper into the skin at my throat. "We're Youngs from Three Willows."

Did you ever try to swallow with a knife pressing on the bump on your throat? Try it sometime. It isn't easy. My clan, the Laus from Phoenix Village, had been feuding with the Youngs of Three Willows ever since our ancestors had settled in neighboring valleys. It was bound to happen, I suppose, since they both had to compete for the same land and water. For a long time my clan had had the upper hand and had bullied the Youngs. But then the Youngs, in just one stroke, had reversed things and were starting to muscle my clan. I knew that my life now depended on choosing my words carefully. "Listen, I'm sure you've got a long list of wrongs—"

Her eyes narrowed and she jabbed down with the

knife, and I could feel a wetness at its tip. "Six years ago you Laus snuck into our valley, killed a woman, and stole most of our rice crop."

I remembered that raid in the fog. I'd been cold and miserable and stumbling through the mud after the others when some girl had almost taken off my head with her hoe. And that girl was . . . "You," I gasped.

"Yes." Her lips were a thin, bloodless line. "I ought to end your miserable, thieving life."

"I was just following orders," I protested.

But the hatred for that raid left very little room for forgiveness in those eyes. "So you think that gives you an excuse to leave an entire village to starve?"

I decided that if she was going to kill me, she might as well hear the truth. "I've heard parts of our clan book about the feud. There's a long list of wrongs on our side too. No one can say who started the fighting."

I readied myself for the downward plunging of the steel, but if anything, she lifted the knife slightly. "Is that true?" The question was directed to the older of the two men and not to me.

"I suppose so." The man limped over. In his hands he held an odd contraption. It was two metal tubes on a long wooden triangle. And I knew it for a gun of strange design, because a regular matchlock would have had a pistol grip. Instead of burning cords of string, there seemed to be iron hammers, and instead of a button, there were two slivers of iron. Around his arm was a cloth of the same red color as mine and the girl's. "At any rate, he also wants to restore the Light."

"You can't trust a Lau." The girl scowled.

He rested the barrels on his left forearm. "I hate to have to quote your brother's letters, but this time he's right: We're each like someone stumbling around in the dark—only we make the darkness for ourselves because we insist on wearing all these blindfolds. Every time we think the most important thing is to be from Phoenix Village or from the Four Districts, we put on a new blindfold. We can't see how much we have in common with other people."

This brother of hers sounded like a pretty wild fellow. The only thing that any of the rebels had in common was that they hated the Manchus more than they distrusted each other.

"Even Foxfire," the girl said stubbornly, "would have said this was an exception."

There was only one person with that fabulous name. Foxfire had been the bold dreamer who'd been among the first to go overseas to a land with a golden mountain—or *America*, as it was called. Others of his clan had copied him, and the riches they had sent back had led to the sudden rise of the Youngs' over ours. Among other things, their sudden wealth had allowed them to buy a weapon made by the demons—the *British*, in this case. That was the way of demons, of course: working as much good fortune for someone as bad.

And suddenly I knew who the older man and the girl were, because there couldn't be another pair like them in the whole of the Middle Kingdom. The older man had to be Foxfire's father, an old warrior called the Gallant, and the girl had to be Foxfire's sister, Cassia—who, some people whispered, was part serpent. I could believe it too. She had this cold, intense look on her face just like a snake trying to figure out if you were prey or not.

"This latest defeat has set me to thinking." The man spoke with deliberate care, as if the thoughts were coming to him right at that moment. "I think that the Light has to be more than a symbolic name. It's the Light within each of us, and that Light is more important than our own prejudices. We have to live the Light. We have to be it."

Encouraged, I went on. "That's right. We ought to be fighting Manchus, not one another." Actually,

I'd had my fill of rebellions, but it seemed like the thing to say.

Maybe I was just a little too quick to agree, because he studied me thoughtfully. "Don't say it unless you really mean it, boy. The Light will come one way or another. No one, not even the Manchus, can stop it."

I remember thinking that this was all I needed: to be captured by a band of fanatics.

The younger man came forward and tugged at the girl's arm. He was a big fellow with huge, callused hands. "We ought to save the speeches for later. Right now let's just get home." He spoke in the clipped, monotonous accent of a Stranger, one of a group of people who had come into our province several centuries ago. Instead of fitting in with everyone else, they had insisted on keeping their own dialect and customs, so they stuck out wherever they settled. And then they had the nerve to compete with the original inhabitants for jobs and land when both were already hard to come by. As a result, there wasn't any love lost between our kind and theirs.

"That's fine by me," I said.

The girl rose and tucked the knife away behind her once again. "But I keep the knife."

"I don't think it would make much difference anyway." I sat up slowly and nodded to the gun. "I've seen matchlocks and even a demon musket, but never anything like that."

"The demons call it a *shotgun*." The man enunciated the last two sounds with great care as if relishing the feeling on his tongue.

I put a hand to my throat and felt the drop of blood there. The cut was hardly more than a pinprick. "Does your son really sit on top of a golden mountain?" I asked the Gallant.

"Hardly." He laughed. He was more forgiving than his daughter, it seemed.

"You Laus must have started shipping men overseas, so you ought to know the truth." The girl gave a cough as more smoke swirled through the windows.

"Yes, but none of them are as wealthy as your brother," I said to her. "Or as influential." I checked my nose, but the blood had already stopped flowing.

"It helps to be one of the first ones." There was a trace of cautious pride in her voice.

Suddenly the Gallant raised his free hand. "Quiet."

We could hear the distant clopping of hooves. "Horsemen." I rubbed at my eyes, which were red from the smoke. "Manchus?"

"Or their puppets." The Gallant gripped his gun. The sound of the hooves grew louder as the horsemen approached the village. "How about giving me back my knife?" I asked the girl.

The girl stared at me suspiciously. "How do I know you won't use it on us?"

"Because the Manchus are killing everyone in sight." I held out my hand.

The girl took out the knife and held it by the blade. "Truce?"

I nodded. "Till we get home."

She threw my knife down centimeters from my foot. "Break that oath and I'll hound you into the underworld and through all your next lives."

"It's a deal." I rose. "So where do we make our stand?"

"Nowhere." The Gallant limped toward the door. The girl went over to support him right away. There was a ragged, bloody slash across his shirt, and through the gap I could see a stained bandage binding his chest. His limp seemed to be from some earlier wound. "I've found a place to hide."

Cassia wrinkled her nose in disgust. "Hide?"

"The Brotherhood has lost one battle, but not the war." The Brotherhood was the secret society of rebels. "We have to be ready to rise up again." He opened the door and peered outside. "Come on—it's all clear."

I followed them over the twisted corpses. Some of

them had been cut down as they ran. Others lay in a headless heap as if they had been executed.

"We should make them pay," Cassia said.

The Gallant looked approvingly over his shoulder at his daughter. "Then let's make sure that you're alive so you can be there to demand that price."

I followed them into a huge privy. It was just a large hole over which two planks had been suspended. I was a farm boy, so I was used to the smell of manure; but I didn't enjoy the prospect of actually diving into it. "In here?"

The Gallant took an oilcloth from the pouch slung over his shoulder and began to wrap up his gun. "It's the one place that they're not going to search thoroughly."

I wrinkled my nose. "Well, as my friend Ducky is always saying, we'll just have to make the best of it."

"Your friend is a wise person." The Gallant looked at his daughter. "I saw a little stand of bamboo. Cut some thin pieces so we can breathe."

When Cassia took a knife from a sheath behind her neck, I had to laugh. "You're a regular arsenal, aren't you?"

"No one's going to surprise *me*." She stepped back outside, and I followed her and almost bumped into her when she stopped abruptly and squatted down. "That's different."

I looked around, but all I could see were corpses and burning houses. "What?"

"This." Her fingertip caressed a delicate white flower as if she were petting the throat of a kitten. "I've never seen anything quite like that."

It was strange to see this girl who'd been brandishing a knife just a moment ago suddenly forget all about war for a flower. Her face had lost that cold, intense, serpentlike look and taken on a softer, more human expression of simple curiosity. "It's just a flower."

It was the wrong thing to say. Her head twisted around and she gave me that same cold, hard look as before—as if I had actually trampled on the flower. "I use them in medicines."

Everything I said or did seemed to rub her the wrong way so I chose my next words with care. "You're a herbalist."

She plucked the flower and tucked it away in her sash before she stood up. "My mother was." As she started on again, she looked at me over her shoulder. "Just what is your name anyway?"

"People call me Squeaky, for my high voice." I

imitated a rusty hinge squeaking and saw her actually smile. "Ah, that's better. For a moment, I thought all you could do was frown."

She gripped four small pieces of bamboo in her hand and chopped them at the base. "The Work is too serious to joke about."

The Work was the word some people called the Revolution. "But if you forget how to laugh, you won't remember when we've finally won. And then what kind of life will we have?"

She made a face as if I'd left a bad taste in her mouth and got up. "The comics are always the first to die." She tossed the words over her shoulder. "And rightly so."

Chapter Two

The Gallant was already standing up to his chest in the pit. "It's not too deep," he tried to encourage us.

But the only encouragement I needed was hearing the sound of Manchu horses. "I'll try anything once," I said, and eased down into the pit.

"Don't forget your bamboo, Tiny." The girl inspected a piece and gave it to the Stranger. "Here, this one's hollow too." After checking another, she climbed down beside her father and handed it to him.

"Do I get the plugged one?" I held out my hand.

She smiled thinly as she passed one on to me. "Don't give me ideas."

We could hear voices in the street. Men were shouting as if they were searching the buildings and announcing that there was no one in there.

The Gallant tilted back his head. "All right," he whispered. "Squat down and be sure that only the top part of the bamboo shows." And he slowly disappeared into the pool until only the tip of the bamboo was visible. Taking a breath, Tiny submerged a moment later.

Copying the other two, Cassia leaned her head back and began to lower herself, but paused to look at me. "The smell doesn't get any better, no matter how long you wait."

"I was counting on new experiences," I said, "but this wasn't one of them."

"Wait till the Manchus take off your head." Setting the bamboo to her lips, Cassia disappeared until only its top was left. Her left hand appeared for a moment while she checked the depth. Satisfied, the hand slipped back into the pool.

So much for all those visions of glory I'd bragged about to Uncle Itchy. He'd really be having a big laugh if he could see me now. Lifting back my head, I put the bamboo in my mouth and took an experimental breath. It was hollow too. I'm afraid that I didn't trust Cassia much.

A man suddenly spoke from right outside the building. Had I waited too long? I quickly closed my eyes and squatted down, touching the top of the bamboo with one hand so that I would know when I had gone down far enough.

My chest felt tight as I took an experimental breath. The air wasn't the sweetest, but it still was air. When I heard the footsteps in the building, my chest felt even tighter. The Manchu circled the pit leisurely. I could only hope that he thought the bamboo was just some debris that had fallen on the surface.

Suddenly I heard a splash. I stiffened, fighting the urge to jump up and see what was going on. There was another splash even closer to me. You're all right, Squeaky, I told myself. Nothing's going to harm you.

Suddenly there was a splash that seemed right behind me, and I felt something sharp and hard cut into my right buttock. I bit down on the bamboo to try to keep from crying out. It had to be a spear blade. I suppose those Manchus wouldn't trust their own grandmothers. Well, maybe I wouldn't either. And then the spear blade was gone. I waited for him to raise the alarm, but I suppose there hadn't been enough resistance, so he hadn't noticed that he'd struck someone. Then, after a moment, though it hurt, it didn't hurt terribly.

I heard the Manchu splash his spear into the pool a couple of more times, and then someone shouted impatiently from the street. The man yelled back some reply, and we heard his footsteps trot out of the building.

A short while later we heard the Manchus gallop away on their horses. And it took only a little longer before I heard the Gallant announce that it was all right to stand up again. He must have stood up to check already.

I rose to see three sticky, messy people grinning at one another. "Well, that's another one we made it through." Cassia started to brush some hair out of her eyes, saw her hand, and thought better of it. "There's nothing wrong that a little water can't cure."

"Not quite." I winced as I stood up. "The Manchu got me."

The Gallant started to wade over to me. "Where?"

I glanced in embarrassment at Cassia. "In a very undignified place."

"You'll be able to walk?" the Gallant asked as if he were genuinely worried.

I took an experimental step. "Yes," I said, but had

to add, "but I don't know if I'll be sitting down for a while."

"That's typical for a Phoenix." Cassia laughed.

"That's enough of that," the Gallant scolded her. "How can we hope to do anything if we can't unite? Every village hates its neighbors."

"And both villages hate the Strangers," the big man added.

"Look at him. He's a child of the T'ang," he lectured her in a teacherlike tone. "Just like you and me and Tiny." The T'ang was a great dynasty some thousand years ago when there was peace and plenty for everyone.

As fierce a warrior as she was, she was more like the prize pupil trying to regain her teacher's favor. "And then," she suggested hopefully, "everyone can get around to hating the Manchus."

I made the mistake of saying, "Maybe there's too much hatred."

Cassia shot a venomous look at me. "Not when it comes to Manchus, you—"

The Gallant interrupted her sternly. "We are still in a state of war with the Manchus. You have to forget the old feuds. Right now his enemies are our enemies."

"Yes, Father." Cassia's mouth squirmed as if she were having a hard time holding back some retort. It seemed that the Phoenixes were next to the Manchus on her hate list.

Her father said, "And he's received an honorable wound from the enemy."

"Yes, Father." She hung her head like some small child.

Her father took a deep breath as if he were about to try to topple a house. "So I want you to apologize for laughing at him." When Cassia's head whipped back rebelliously, he held up his index finger. "He's an ally now."

I cleared my throat. "It's . . . unh . . . not necessary."

"No," the Gallant said as he kept his eyes on his daughter, "this is something that Cassia has to do as much for herself as for you."

I tried to clean my hands by rubbing them together. "As for that, it's more important to look ahead and not at the past."

The Gallant spoke in a firm but gentle voice. "We have to be able to cooperate together if we're ever going to drive out the Manchus. If you can't realize that, there's no place for you in the Work."

That threat, apparently, was too much for Cassia. "I'm sorry," she mumbled to me.

In all my years I'd never met anyone quite like her. In fact most people I knew didn't care about the Work—let alone being expelled from it. There was a streak of the wild dreamer in both Foxfire's sister and his father. "I can guess what it costs you to say that."

She gave me a suspicious glance. "What do you mean by that?"

Her father clicked his tongue in annoyance. "I'd never thought I'd say this, but sometimes it's possible to be too serious. Sometimes kind words are just kind words."

It was Tiny who got us back to more practical matters. "Right now, it's more important to wash up."

With Tiny's help, I got out of the pit. Though he didn't seem to say much, I liked the big man. He gave off a safe, rocklike feeling—as if you could always trust him to protect you from behind and to support you.

While Cassia took a bucket of water into a nearby house to wash up, we stood by the well.

The Gallant slipped off his shirt. "You have to understand my daughter. Her mother died while I was off fighting a war, and she and her little brother had a hard time of it. And when I came back she took over and ran everything."

I stripped off my shirt. "That's a lot of responsibility."

"Maybe too much." With a push of his fingers, the Gallant knocked the bucket into the well. "She never had time to be a child."

"Maybe these aren't times for childish people." I put my shirt on a rock so I could wash it later.

When he heard the bucket splash, the Gallant began to haul it back up. "And then she got involved in the Work. We've given so much to it and gotten so little back in return. Well, it's made her a little bitter—even suspicious of people. I suppose it's my fault."

He looked guilty about that. He was now more a worried father than a famous warrior. I leaned over to add my strength to his. "She's probably had a lot of disappointments, and you're not the one who did all of that."

The Gallant paused as he studied me. "But I could have encouraged her to play more and make friends." He began to haul up on the rope again.

"That was as much her choice as yours." Together we balanced the brimming bucket on the rim of the well.

"Well, my daughter may not make friends easily, but when she does, she's ready to die for them." He couldn't help chuckling. "So she has to be serious even about friendship."

"That makes her a rare person," I said, and was glad when the Gallant smiled.

"And worth knowing," Tiny added.

While we cleaned up, Tiny inspected my "honorable" wound as he slid the thong of a little wooden Buddha around his neck. "It's not bad. It's just a flesh wound." The words came from him ponderously—not that he was stupid, but the sounds just seemed to weigh heavily on his tongue. That made me appreciate his efforts even more.

"But it should leave an amusing scar." The Gallant clapped me on the shoulder. "Now you've got something to show people when they ask you what happened to you during the uprising."

I wrung out my shirt. "It won't surprise them that the wound's behind me."

The Gallant put his own trousers back on. "And I think you'd believe them." He wagged a finger at me. "There's more to you than you or those others think. Someone else might have gotten up because of the shock and the pain and given us away to the Manchus."

I straightened out my shirt so I could put it on. "Maybe I was just too scared to do anything."

"I think you have the right instincts. You just don't act on them." The Gallant put a hand behind my neck so that I couldn't look away from his eyes. "Listen to me, boy. The Light is more than a pun on the name of an old dynasty, just as the Darkness is more than a pun on the name of the Manchus. There's a whole world of darkness around us that's trying to put out the Light in each of us. There's a light in you. If you could only learn to let it out, you could do anything."

It was strange. I hardly knew the man; and yet, for a moment, I thought I could see the Light burning inside him—like a candle flaring into life within a paper lantern. And I felt as if a little spark of that Light passed between the two of us.

Tiny cleared his throat as if he were pleased with the Gallant's thoughts. He seemed to be a man of few words, but he meant them when he did speak. "So restore the Light."

"Banish the Darkness," I agreed.

"Maybe we could continue the discussion on our way out of here," Cassia said, and broke the mood.

"We were heading to the river to get on a boat," the Gallant explained. "What were your plans?"

"Father," Cassia gasped in disapproval. I guess she didn't like letting an enemy like me know their plans.

After that inspiring little speech on the Light, I would have liked to have said something noble and chivalric, but all I could do was confess, "I'm just trying to save my head."

But I was wrong if I thought the Gallant was going to make fun of me. "That's reasonable enough. I wish I could tell you how many times that was the only idea in my head when the Manchus were chasing me."

From the corner of my eye, I was aware of Cassia glaring at me, but I kept my eyes on the Gallant. "You've done this sort of thing before?"

"I've been fighting Manchus all my life," he boasted. "And I'll keep on doing it until they get tired and give up. Now let's get going—if we want to fight them some other day."

As we trudged along the path out of the village, I fell into step beside Tiny. "Is she always so touchy?" I asked him in Stranger.

Tiny looked at me in surprise. "You understand my dialect?" he asked me, also in Stranger. He sounded grateful to be speaking his own tongue.

"A little," I answered. "There's a Stranger called Ducky who's been like a second father to me."

Tiny was all smiles. "Oh, yes, Ducky. We used to look forward to seeing him before he retired." Tiny seemed more comfortable talking in his own dialect, so the formerly quiet man was full of words—as if he hadn't been able to hold a real conversation for ages.

"You saw him perform?" I asked.

"I don't think there was ever a better acrobat." Tiny looked up at the clouds as if he could see Ducky there. "He just seemed to fly through the air—and he was so funny, too." He glanced shyly back at me to see if I was laughing at his attempt to describe Ducky. When he saw that I wasn't, he seemed even more grateful than before. "But I had no idea he was a neighbor."

I clasped my hands behind my back. "It's what comes of never crossing the ridgetop between our villages. He got tired of the road, so he settled in our village."

Tiny gave a grunt—as if he knew what it meant to turn to a Stranger for friendship: that I was probably as much an outcast in my own village as he was in his. "He might just as well live in Canton for all the good it does me."

Cassia dropped back beside us. "What are you two talking about?"

Tiny waved his hand at me with proud excitement. "He knows the best acrobat in the world."

"More than knows," I boasted. "He's been teaching me." As we had walked, I had felt better about my wound. It only stung every now and then, so I felt up to trying out one of Duck's tricks. Raising my hands over my head, I launched myself through the air in a cartwheel.

Ducky had always told me to try to be a tree growing from the ground. I tried to do that now as I turned upside down and my hands touched the ground. At the same time, my legs were already swinging over to touch the ground again.

Even though Ducky was some forty years older than me, he could still manage a series of cartwheels up and down the main village street; but I'd never managed more than a half dozen. This time I didn't even make it past three. Intent on impressing them, I swung my legs too hard, so I couldn't recover and wound up landing right on my war wound.

The Gallant and Tiny were busy shouting, "Good, good," but Cassia was only frowning. "I hope you didn't open up your wound again."

I picked myself up carefully from the road, waiting for some moment of pain, but there wasn't any. "No, I think that part of me is harder than most."

"What else can you do?" the Gallant called cheerfully.

"I can juggle—a little." As we walked along, I looked around for something suitable, but I didn't see anything.

Cassia, however, had her hands on her hips, and she was looking at me as if I were the biggest fool. "You ought to spend more time learning how to fight and less time learning how to be a clown."

I made a face. "That would have meant getting beat up by my cousin Lumpy most of the time. He was the best at the martial arts, and he liked to prove it to everyone."

Cassia lowered her hands thoughtfully. "Lumpy was the bully who gave you that scar." She'd surprised me by remembering. I'd have thought she'd be so busy trying to save the country, she wouldn't have time for an individual's concerns.

"That's him, all right. It was easier to make friends another way." It made me nervous to talk about myself that way. I tried to hide it by testing my hair. The sun had nearly dried it.

Cassia cocked her head to one side as if she were hearing about some strange, foreign custom. "By making people laugh?"

With a start, I realized that she was studying me the way she had the flower. It made me feel both flattered and uncomfortable at the same time. "I think Ducky felt sorry for this odd, goofy little boy that the others all made fun of." I reminded myself that I didn't have anything to be ashamed of. "So Ducky showed me how to make them laugh *with* me instead of *at* me."

But that admission only seemed to puzzle Cassia more. She motioned over her shoulder toward Canton. "Then why did you go there?"

I scuffed the dirt as I walked. "I guess I wanted to be taken more seriously." I was beginning to feel like I was a fly caught in glue that she was examining; and I'd had enough of that. I halted abruptly and, bringing my heels together sharply, waved a hand at my chest as if I were presenting myself. "So far I haven't done too good a job, have I?"

But instead of chuckling or at least smiling as I thought she would, Cassia frowned in disapproval.

I thought it was because she didn't understand. "You know, my war wound." As I started to walk along again, I waved exaggeratedly toward the wound and then back toward the village. "You know, the pit."

But Cassia had understood me, all right. "You don't have to be onstage now." I was startled to see that her face had again taken on that softer expression she'd had when she'd been examining the flower.

People usually reacted to my clowning in a very different way. Cassia was . . . well . . . so relentlessly earnest. She kept prodding me in unexpected ways, so all I could do was speak the truth. "It's habit, I guess."

She hugged herself. "But it's not a habit that you're happy with—or you would have stayed home doing exactly what you're doing now."

She certainly knew how to unsettle me. Flustered, I began to wind my hair back into a queue. "I don't know. Maybe it's hopeless."

"No." She regarded me quietly. "I know someone who went away just like you did—only he found what he was looking for. And more."

As he limped along, the Gallant looked over his shoulder at us sorrowfully. "Go ahead. Tell him how I drove your little brother to *America*." I think that he used the demon name for that country. "Tell him how we were always arguing." He spoke as if it were some penance to tell every stranger about his sins.

Cassia clicked her tongue in exasperation, as if this

were an old argument between them. "Will you stop punishing yourself, Father? Foxfire wanted to go overseas."

But the Gallant was determined to be hard on himself. "But I didn't give him much choice by disowning him."

"But you've accepted him again as your son," Cassia tried to console him. "It won't be like it was before. You're a lot more openminded now."

"I try." The Gallant sighed and stroked his hair. "But some of those notions that he gets from the demons are just too outrageous for me. He doesn't think it's so bad if someone doesn't have a clan or a family."

"No clan?" I gaped. "But that's like . . . like trying to stand on thin air." I tried to picture it, but it was too frightening to spend much time on—like picturing myself climbing a ladder of knives.

"Some of them aren't so ridiculous, though," Cassia assured me.

"Well," I admitted, "at least he has something to show for it—which is more than I ever will."

"There are other dreams," Cassia argued.

I went on twisting my hair. "I'm not your brother."

To my surprise, Cassia pushed my hands aside.

"Honestly, I think you're worse. At least my little brother could braid his hair without getting it all tangled up." Her hands were strong and sure as they began to pull my hair into three thick strands.

I leaned my head back to make it easier for her as we walked along. "There are some people who are just destined to find those dreams. And then there are folks like me who never will. I'm always going to be the village clown."

Cassia tugged lightly at my hair as if she were holding reins. "And anyway, there are worse things than being a clown." A wistful note crept into her voice.

I tried to turn around. "Such as?"

She tapped one fistful of hair against my shoulder to keep me looking straight ahead. "I think it's harder to be funny than it is to be serious."

This time I craned my head back so that I could look at her. "You're not joking, are you?"

She gave me a shy, sad smile. "I wish I were. I've never, never been able to tell a joke right. And then another person can come along and tell the same joke and everyone will be laughing."

I studied her face for a moment; and though it seemed upside down from my perspective, she seemed perfectly serious—as always, I guess. If she was as earnest then as she was now, I could see how the somber, serious little girl might stand out as much as odd, dumb little Squeaky. We each had our way of protecting ourselves. I had my clowning, and she had that cold, serpentlike look and that hard, relentless logic of hers. I was actually beginning to feel sorry for her—I, the clown. "It seems a shame that you're going to be condemned to be somber the rest of your life. We should give lessons to one another. You could teach me how to be serious, and I could teach you how to tell a joke."

She seemed surprised—as if she had never considered that possibility. "I don't know if joking is something you can teach," she warned, and added in a big-sister voice, "Now stand up straight while you walk."

I obeyed quickly. "We've got a long trip ahead of us." I winced as she pulled a bit too hard.

"Sorry," Cassia said absently.

The Gallant turned sideways so he could look at us as he limped along. He seemed a little more relaxed now that we had escaped the Manchus, and ready to indulge his daughter. "It would pass the time for all of us."

Cassia still seemed to hesitate: but then some sudden impulse seemed to overtake her. Maybe she recognized that we were alike in some ways. Whatever the reasons, she gave a light, wary tug at my hair—as if she had just struck a bargain, and not a very good one at that, for a half dozen ducks. "All right. It's a deal."

Chapter Three

The beach was empty when we reached the riverbank, so we followed it for a kilometer before we
found the docks. It was just a little riverboat with a
high stern and bow, and every bit of its deck seemed
to be jammed with people, hens, and baskets, as
everyone tried to get away from the bloodthirsty
Manchus and their dogs.

There were even more people crowded at the foot
of the narrow, rickety dock. They were trying to get
to the boat, but three sailors were keeping them back
with prods of their bamboo sticks. Without looking

at Cassia, the Gallant held a hand out toward her. "We're going to need money to get on."

She touched her blouse at a spot just beneath her throat. "But that was meant to be a souvenir."

The Gallant continued to hold out his palm. "Foxfire can always send another."

But Cassia kept her hand there. "But he had to save up a long time, and it must have been hard to send us this one."

The Gallant wriggled his fingers. "It won't do us any good if we're dead."

"I guess so." Reluctantly, Cassia slid her hand into her blouse and extracted a small pouch that hung around her neck. The pouch was embroidered and looked as if it might have held some charm or amulet against evil—and in a way, I guess it did. When she opened the mouth of the pouch, I saw the glint of gold.

"You've got a gold coin there?" I asked breathlessly.

"Twenty *American dollars*," Cassia declared proudly. "That's more than a field hand could expect to earn in a season." She held it so I could see it.

"What kind of bird is that?" I pointed at a big-beaked, squinting bird on the front.

"An *eagle*." The Gallant closed his fist around the

coin. He glanced at me. "That should get the four of us on a boat."

"They aren't likely to give us change," I warned.

"There are more important things than money." The Gallant began to study the pushing, shouting crowd at the foot of the dock like a dog looking for the way through a dense clump of shrubbery.

Tiny pumped his arms experimentally. "Let me earn my share of the fare." And he plunged into the crowd.

"Keep close." Cassia motioned for us to follow her as she caught hold of Tiny's shirt.

He didn't exactly shove his way into the crowd; it was more like he lifted it out of his way.

"He really is strong," I said, staring after the big man.

"He used to be a blacksmith," Cassia explained. She had taken hold of her father's wrist, and he had taken mine in turn. Meter by meter, we snaked our way through that crowd until we got to the front.

"Get back." A sailor in a dirty rag of a turban struck Tiny across the head. He stood there, dazed for a moment.

"Leave this to me now." The Gallant squeezed past his daughter and then Tiny.

"Don't push," the sailor ordered the Gallant, and tried to knock him back with a stick. But the Gallant caught one end of the stick and with a neat twist of his wrist forced the sailor to bend at an awkward angle until the sailor had to let go of the stick.

The captain was a tall man in an embroidered vest and exotic slippers that curved upward. "I believe that's ours." He held out his hand for the stick.

The Gallant gave it back. "We want passage on your boat."

The captain handed the stick to his indignant sailor. "How many?"

"Four." The Gallant held up his fingers to emphasize the number.

The captain shook his head. "You can see how low the boat's riding in the water. I can take only three more."

I suppose I should have volunteered to stay. Cassia even turned around to look at me. But when I kept my mouth shut, she only curled up the corners of her mouth into a contemptuous smile. In the meantime, though, the Gallant hadn't given up.

"It's too dangerous," the captain was insisting.

It was Cassia's turn now. She stood on tiptoe so that she could look over her father's shoulder. "You look like a man of the world, captain. You know how much a *dollar* will buy."

"It won't buy me anything if my boat sinks." The captain began surveying the crowd for two more likely candidates. "And I've heard enough promises this morning."

"But my brother lives overseas, and he sent this to us." When Cassia nudged the Gallant, he held up the gold coin. And I could have blessed Foxfire a hundred times.

The captain stared at the coin. "Is that all gold?"

"Try it." The Gallant offered the coin to the captain.

He bit it and examined it to see if the gold had only coated some lead coin, but it was genuine. "Get on board," he said.

The Gallant stepped onto the dock and waved Tiny, Cassia, and me past. "Hurry, children."

It was difficult to find footing on the boat. The swift river currents made it jerk and tug at the two lines that bound it to the head of the dock—as if it were some horse eager to be off. What made it even more difficult to stand on the boat was that there was hardly any room on deck to stand—let alone sit. And the people already there had staked out their territory. They weren't particularly happy about having to make room for four more people. "Watch it," one complained, and slapped at Tiny's leg.

"Sorry." The big man began to edge his way to the other side of the boat.

In the meantime the captain and his crew were slowly retreating toward the boat while the rest of the crowd shouted and shoved even more desperately. They would have made it in good order if a plume of dust hadn't appeared in the distance on the road.

"Horsemen," someone yelled in a shrill, panicky voice. And the next moment people began to scream. The crowd dissolved like a clump of mud dumped into water. People darted away to hide in the shrubs. Others tried to force their way between the sailors and were clubbed to the dock.

The captain jumped on board the boat, heedless of who he stepped on. "Cast off the lines," he bellowed.

But the sailors had all they could do to fight off the panicked crowd now. One of them was heaved off the dock into the water, another was knocked unconscious, while a third tried to protect his friend.

And all the time we could only watch helplessly as the plume of dust came closer.

"Hurry—the lines." The captain was forcing his way toward the rudder.

"Someone has to help them." The Gallant began to slide his odd-looking bundle from his shoulder.

"This requires someone with faster feet." Cassia stopped him and looked straight at me.

Her expression seemed to say that now was the time I could prove I was more than a clown. But at that moment it seemed more important to live. "They'll manage." I tried to shrug lamely.

"Then I'll help them cast off the lines." Before we could stop her, Cassia was shoving her way across the crowded deck toward the dock.

I got up, intending to follow Cassia; but like all my best intentions, I just couldn't carry it out.

"I'll go with her," Tiny finally said, and left.

The Gallant glanced at me and seemed disappointed that I hadn't gone as well.

"I'm sorry" was all I could murmur. "I guess you ought to know what a coward I am. I hide from every battle."

He studied me for a moment. "Don't be so hard on yourself." He cradled his bundle in his arms.

"Sometime you'll reach down into yourself and you'll find what you need." And he began to limp after the other two.

But it was so hard to move on deck that Cassia had barely made it to the dockside when the horsemen clopped up to the dock itself. The crowd stopped fighting and began to back away cautiously.

It wasn't Manchus at all, but eight rebels with dirty red armbands. Most of them were riding double, and from the way they clung to one another and to their mounts, they looked like they were more used to sitting on slow, plodding water buffalo than on fast horses. Each of them had some kind of clinking bundle that I assumed was loot. And each of them had a look that suggested it wouldn't be wise to defy them.

The one remaining sailor looked at them and then threw his bamboo stick away as useless.

The leader trotted forward—or rather, his horse did and he just tried to stay on top of it as best he could. Even so, I didn't feel like laughing at the man. His whole body gave the impression of a taut rope that, once snapped, would whip about in a deadly way.

And yet there was something terribly familiar about the man; and when I saw that his black trousers had been tucked into his white stockings in the northern style, I knew it was the mercenary we'd called Dusty. He'd fought for our village for a while against the Youngs. "In the name of the Revolution, we're commandeering this boat. Everybody off."

"You've got horses." Cassia made shooing motions as if the rebels were only loud, noisy ducks. "Ride away."

Dusty climbed down off his horse as if it were a big boulder. "So it's the little tiger." He looked around the crowd. "If you're here, your father can't be far away."

By that time the Gallant had joined Tiny and his daughter. He had already loosened the oilcloth that covered his shotgun. "Here I am."

Dusty held his cutlass menacingly over his head. "We have some unfinished business, old man." I don't think I've ever seen anyone move quite as fast as him. It was more like he was shot from a bow than actually running.

But the Gallant refused to back down. He shook the oilcloth off so that it fluttered to the deck, and then he raised his gun so that the base of the wooden triangle was against his shoulder. Pointing the barrels toward Dusty, he pulled one of the two slender, tonguelike bits of metal.

[43]

Dusty threw himself to the side just as a hammer fell at the rear of one tube and the air seemed to explode with a roar. Black smoke rose around the Gallant as he tried to aim the other barrel at Dusty, but the rebel flung himself into the crowd on the dock. People shouted and screamed as Dusty disappeared among them.

The Gallant nodded to the one remaining sailor. "Cast off the lines."

While that sailor cautiously walked toward the first line, the sailor who had been knocked unconscious crawled onto the boat. At the same time the third sailor, dripping water from the river, clambered onto it.

Dusty suddenly thrust his way to the front of the crowd. His arm was hooked around the neck of a terrified, screaming child. "Let's make a deal, old man. You can go too."

The Gallant watched the wet sailor grab a pole and get ready to shove off. "I prefer the present ship's company."

The first line was cast off, and the ship's bow began to swing away from the dock.

A desperate edge crept into Dusty's voice. "We'll share our loot with you."

"I've a son living in mountains all of gold," the

Gallant said scornfully. "What do I need with your trinkets?"

"Virtue is easy for the rich." Dusty shoved the child away and, pulling a knife from his sleeve, sent it hissing through the air. It caught the sailor in the back as he was about to release the last line. Spinning around, he fell into the river with a cry.

Suddenly the Gallant swung his gun down. He set the base of the wooden triangle against his shoulder and fired at the last cable holding the boat to the shore.

"Get him," Dusty roared frantically.

The cable just seemed to disintegrate under the blast. But the roar of the gun hid the sound of the spear that sank, the next moment, in the Gallant's chest. His mouth jerked open and his eyes widened and his back arched so that the spear shaft seemed to rise.

"Father." Cassia would have caught him, but he thrust the gun into her hands.

"Remember—" And then he fell backward onto the deck, his eyes wide and open.

"Don't let the boat get away." Dusty raced forward to scoop up his sword.

The sailor with the pole was shoving frantically, trying to help the current pull us away from the dock.

But in the meantime, Cassia had fallen to her knees and was digging into the oilcloth pouch still hanging from the Gallant's shoulder. She dug out two cardboard cylinders.

"Hurry, you fools," Dusty called over his shoulder to his followers.

With a well-practiced flick of her fingers, Cassia touched a lever that made the gun break in half. People all around her were screaming in terror, sure that they were going to die under the looters' swords. But they might just have been so many pigs squealing over slops for all the attention that Cassia gave them. She slid one cylinder into the barrel and lined up a pin at the base of the cylinder with a notch in the barrel. She didn't try to load the other cylinder, but cracked the barrels back onto the wooden stock.

Still kneeling, she whirled around and brought the gun up to her shoulder as Dusty and his looters thumped over the old wooden boards of the dock, shouting their war cries. When she fired, she was almost knocked backward by the force of the gun. More black smoke wreathed the boat as the war cries changed to screams of pain. Of the eight men charging toward us, none of them was left on his feet. But Dusty was rising from the dock. He must have dropped down just when Cassia fired.

"Come on. Come on." A tearful Cassia was frantically trying to reload her gun again for another shot at him; but as fast as she was, the river was even faster. By the time she was ready, we were twenty meters from the dock and Dusty was gone—his horse once again raising plumes of dust behind it.

Chapter Four

I squatted down beside the bulwark where Tiny and
Cassia were kneeling. All her rhetoric, all her revo-
lutionary principles, weren't doing Cassia much good
now. "I'm sorry."

She turned from looking at the riverbank and stared
at me as if I were a bug that had just crawled from
between the planks. "Oh, go away."

I would have liked nothing better than to slink
away, but I couldn't. "The captain says that we have
to dispose of your father's body."

She whirled around, her hand tightening on the gun. "I'm taking him home to Three Willows."

I nodded toward the sun. "Think of the heat."

"His passage is paid," she insisted.

I held my palm out and curled my fingers as if I could squeeze some sense into her that way. "I didn't know your father that long, but I think he would have put your life before his burial. Even if you did get him to shore, you'd have to put him in a coffin and try to get back to your village. And you've got to put as much distance between yourself and the Manchus as you can."

She flung her hand at the air. "I'll worry about that myself. Just leave us alone."

"See here. You have to be fair to the rest of—" an old woman began to scold her.

"Fair? My father and mother devoted their lives to the Work, and what did they ever get? Nothing." She twisted her head around to take in the whole boat to see if there was anyone foolish enough to contradict her. "You might complain about the Manchus, but you never did anything about it. My father deserves a hero's burial—not to be dumped over the side like garbage."

I tapped my fingers against the bulwark. "The

Manchus are looking for our heads. You've got to travel light now."

She slapped the butt of the gun. "I'll find a way."

I nodded to the gun. "That's a very deadly machine, but it's not going to carry your father back to your village." I softened my voice. "He died so you could live. Don't complicate things."

She gave a start as if someone had just poked a dagger between her shoulder blades. "I don't know. I just don't know." She passed a hand over her forehead, and for a moment she seemed to be what she looked: more like a young woman than some stern warrior.

The captain started to force his way through the crowd on the deck. "The boat's overloaded—"

Her head snapped back and her hand tightened around the gun. "Whose fault is that?" She looked at him as if she were ready to shoot him and dump *him* over the side.

The captain froze. "Now let's not be hasty."

"No, of course not." When I motioned him back, he seemed glad of an excuse to retreat. "Listen to me," I coaxed Cassia. "This isn't the way your father would have wanted you to honor his memory— frightening a boatload of people."

"What would you know about it?" she demanded; but she sounded less sure.

"Not much," I was quick to say, and then I just kept talking—which my uncle Itchy would have said I did well. Despite the gun and all her tough talk, she was still frightened and very much alone. In her own way she was like a hurt little cat that was hiding in a hole and clawing and biting anyone who tried to reach in.

In the end, it was gentleness that wheedled her out of her hole. "What would you have done if your father had died in battle?"

"Buried him." She ran a finger up and down the barrels of the gun. "But then I would have come back for him."

I shifted one leg that was beginning to cramp up. "If the battle had gone against us, there wouldn't have been time to do that. Or even if there had, you might have lost the marker. This isn't any different from dying in battle."

Tiny cleared his throat. "He's right, you know."

"But it just isn't fair." Suddenly her head dipped and I was surprised to see two drops fall from her cheeks onto the deck. With a start, I realized that she was crying. I hadn't known she was capable of it.

"Anytime I get close to someone, they go away. First Mother. Then Foxfire. Now Father." She gripped the gun as if it could help her now, but of course it couldn't. Poor Cassia. All her fighting ability couldn't help her fight the loneliness.

And I was feeling just as helpless. I wanted to do something for her, but for once all my jokes wouldn't do me any good. I wanted to hug her or at least pat her on the back, but I didn't dare touch her. Instead, I could only lower my voice even more. "But your brother will come back."

"Even if I wrote him today and he could wind up all his business, it would probably take him half a year to come back." She added doubtfully, "And I'm not sure he would."

Desperately, I tried another tack. "Well, you still have the Work."

She straightened at the magical word. "Yes, *we* can carry on his fight."

"It's what he would have wanted," I encouraged her.

She ran her sleeve over her eyes. "For all of us." She gave me a grudging nod of approval. "Father may have been right after all. Maybe a Phoenix can be an ally."

I wanted to put this adventure behind me as quickly

as I could. Uncle Itchy's fields were miserable little scraps of dirt that we had to fight for every crop. But that life, though hard, wasn't this terrifying madness that I had just gone through. "Well, I—" I began. But she looked up at me sharply; and for the life of me, I couldn't refuse as I wanted to do. I wanted her to think at least a little good of me. Instead, all I could do was stammer lamely, "I—I'm not all that brave."

Under her thoughtful gaze I felt like a fat river carp that was being neatly trimmed. "No," she said after a while. "I don't suppose you are." She laid her gun down. "But you can do what you can. And you can start by helping us with my father." As she folded her father's arms over his chest, she called to the captain, "Do you have any weights?"

It took only a few moments for a sailor to bring weights to us, along with some heavy rope. But Cassia wouldn't allow him to help us tie the weights on. Then she smoothed back her father's hair and fussed with his torn, dirty shirt for a moment. "The Work will go on," she promised.

Then she and I took her father by his shoulders and Tiny grabbed his ankles. Someone nearby began to mumble a prayer, and I looked at Cassia to see if she wanted to pray; but her mouth was a tight, bitter line. We heaved her father up—it was a surprise what a heavy load he had become, but somehow we managed to raise him to the railing.

The muddy green water of the river slid by, slapping and churning noisily at the sides of the boat. And I thought again of what he had said—that there was more to me than I thought. "I hope you're right," I murmured.

And then we slid the body over. It splashed into the water and sank quickly.

Chapter Five

We washed up with water drawn by buckets from the river; but the three of us were too tired to do much talking—so were most of the other passengers, for that matter, and we passed a quiet night. The next morning we found the river port of Tiger Hill jammed with a small fleet of boats. It seemed as if everyone were trying to escape to safety. And the streets that led from the docks were crowded with shouting men.

"What's going on?" I muttered anxiously.

"I just want to get home to my wife and son." Tiny

sighed in exasperation. "And then I only want to be left alone."

"Well, I'm not going to wait for trouble to find me." Cassia began to unwrap the oilcloth from around her gun.

However, one of the sailors shook his head. "I know those buildings where the crowds are. They handle men going overseas."

Cassia slowly lowered the cloth back over the gun. "To the land of the golden mountain?" That was what people called the country of *America*.

The sailor shrugged as the boat slipped by one full dock after another. "With the Manchus acting this crazy, it's smarter for a man to get out of the country."

Cassia began rewrapping her gun. "They're fools. They're just jumping from the wolf's claws into the wolf's mouth." I remembered that she had a brother overseas.

The sailor readied a loop of cable. "They might as well get rich while they're doing it."

Cassia jerked the cloth tight. "It's not all that easy."

The sailor gripped the cable stubbornly, unwilling to give up on his dream. "But I've got a cousin who had a friend—"

"Who made a fortune." Cassia wearily settled the

[56]

bundle on her lap. "I know, I know. Everyone always tells you about someone who got rich. But they never tell you about all the many people who barely scratch out a living there."

A woman turned around. "But they say the gold is all over the ground." Other people around us were nodding their heads; and, encouraged, she began pantomiming scooping up handfuls of gold. "All you have to do is pick it up."

Cassia sighed as she looked around at all the hopeful faces. She had obviously had to do this before. "You won't believe me when I tell you, but that land doesn't give up its riches that easily."

The woman lifted her chin like some stubborn, defiant little child. "We won't know until we try."

"That's right," the sailor chimed in.

Cassia slapped a hand against the railing. "What's wrong with you people? You'd rather chase some wild dream than face up to what has to be done: Throw out the Manchus."

The sailor rose as the boat finally neared an open berth. "The rebels tried that, and look what happened."

Cassia grabbed hold of his arm and wrenched him back angrily. "My father died to save your hides."

A little old lady rose. She barely kept her grip on the squealing little pig in her arms. "Oh, quit your troublemaking. We're sick of your kind."

Cassia's eyes narrowed. "My kind? My kind? Well, my kind is dying trying to make the world better for your kind."

"Will you shut up!" the exasperated captain yelled. "We want to dock."

A chorus of voices quickly agreed, and there were even angry fists shaken at her. Cassia looked about uncertainly, as if she weren't sure what to say, but she wasn't about to back down either. "You ungrateful fools are going to listen to the truth whether you like it or not." It was hard to hear what else she was saying, because everyone else around us was shouting angrily.

I slapped the back of my hand against Tiny's arm. It was like hitting a tree. "You'd better quiet her down before she starts a riot."

Tiny shook his head helplessly. "She's even better at starting fights than she is at ending them." He rose, balling his hands into big, hammerlike fists—as if the only thing he could think about doing was to help Cassia in the upcoming fight.

People were really starting to turn ugly. Cassia had this anxious, uncomfortable look on her face—as if she were on a branch that was beginning to break under her weight and all she knew how to do was to go farther and farther out. Her principles were at stake, I guess. And Cassia had never backed down from a fight in her life.

So, at a certain risk to my own safety, I got up and touched her arm. "This isn't doing us any good. They ought to care, but unfortunately they don't. And no amount of arguing is going to change that. You have to know what material works with your audience."

She whirled around in disbelief. "You idiot. I'm not trying to tell jokes now." And she gave me a little shove.

Well, if she had to pick a fight with anyone, it might as well be harmless old Squeaky rather than a boatload of frightened, frustrated people. Even though she hadn't pushed me very hard, I flung out my arms and raised one leg so that I was standing like a stork. "Who-o-o-oa," I screeched. Opening my eyes wide in mock fright, I started to lean forward.

People immediately raised their hands to catch me; but I just hovered there, flailing my arms in the air and making odd howling noises—just as my friend Ducky had taught me. Once people saw that I wasn't going to fall, their alarm changed to amusement. I even heard a few chuckles.

[59]

So did Cassia. She grabbed hold of my collar. "Will you quit clown—"

"Who-o-o-oa." With a kick, I rose in the air; and then I did a quick series of hops as I whipped my head back and forth—as if all this were coming from Cassia's violent shaking. I'm afraid that she was perfect for setups.

"What—?" she said in alarm, and let go.

And, of course, I went on hopping and shaking my head and howling, "Who-o-o-oa."

People were laughing openly now. Cassia stood there for a moment, her cheeks turning redder and redder; and finally, because she could think of nothing else to do, she plopped down on the deck abruptly.

When the boat nosed into the wharf, it gave a little jerk; and I used that as an excuse to finally sit down, flinging my arms and legs up in the air. "Good, good," people were saying now; and, as the sailors ran the gangplank onto the dock, they began to get ready to disembark.

Cassia gave me one of her hard, serpentlike looks. "Don't you ever interrupt me again."

I was still getting back my breath. "Fine. Next time you go ahead and fight a boatload of people."

She considered that for a moment. "Well, maybe I did get carried away a little."

"You can't fight everyone, or you'll wear yourself out," I pointed out to her.

She looked away self-consciously. "It's just that once I got started, I didn't know how to stop."

"Except one way." I leaned back on my hands. "If ever someone needed to know how to tell a joke, it's you."

She bit her lip and curled the corners of her mouth up in a slight smile. "Well, I have to admit that clowning does have its uses sometimes." That was more than I ever thought I'd hear her admit. She was definitely becoming more human the longer I stayed with her.

Tiny lowered an anxious hand to me. When I took it, he lifted me into the air as if I were a doll. "Let's get started for home. I want to see my family."

Cassia rose, and stepped back almost immediately as a man, bent over with a cage of chickens on his back, staggered on by. She looked sad—as if she were remembering her father, and I felt sorry for her. "I suppose you do too," she said to me.

While I didn't feel the same sense of urgency that Tiny did, I was finding it interesting traveling in their company. I motioned Tiny to head for the gangplank. "Not me. All I've got is my uncle, and he doesn't have much use for me."

Cassia glanced at me as she slipped past. "You don't have any parents?"

"No." I followed her across the deck. "They died when I was a child. And my uncle Itchy got stuck with me."

She paused in the line at the gangplank. "Everyone should have a family that cares."

I pulled at my shirt collar uncomfortably. "That sounds great. Where do I buy one? I'd like—"

She turned slowly on her heel and looked straight at me, and the other jokes just died inside of me. "You don't have to turn everything into a joke, you know. People will like you when you're serious, too."

I think I know how a turtle feels when a predator finally breaks through its shell. There's no place left to hide. "I've managed so far," I said defensively.

"You don't have to just *manage* through life. You've got a lot of good qualities." She crossed the rickety wooden gangplank as if it were made of rigid steel.

It took me a little longer to reach the dock. "My uncle Itchy would argue with that notion."

Almost immediately I got bumped by a man carrying a basket at either end of a pole. "Watch it, idiot." With difficulty he started to maneuver around us.

Cassia took my sleeve as if I were a small child.

"Come on. There's no future in being a roadblock."

Pretending to be astounded, I let my jaw drop. "I thought you said you couldn't tell a joke."

"Did I?" Poor Cassia looked like she didn't know whether to be pleased or to feel guilty. "You must be a better teacher than I thought."

I rubbed my stomach. "Well, your teacher's hungry."

I seemed to appeal to some big-sisterly impulse. "We can take care of that." She nodded to Tiny. "Tiny, we need a path."

While Tiny obligingly led the way through the mob, I let her tug me along. "I don't have any money," I warned.

She halted beside a little wineshop, where a servant was taking down the shutters. "Let me take care of that." She caught hold of Tiny's shoulder. "This is the place we stopped at."

"When you were going to—?" I began to ask, when she shot a warning look at me.

"The recent festivities," she said.

I looked around the busy street and realized that there could be spies and informers all around. "Yes, the . . . uh . . . party."

The owner was a small bald man with tufts of hair

like grass growing from underneath the sides of a rock. He was busy washing off the top of a table. "We're not open yet."

"But we've come such a long way." Cassia let go of my sleeve and touched a fingertip to a puddle of water that lay beneath his cleaning rag. Quickly she drew a line of water across the table and then a second and a third.

The owner dragged his damp rag across the lines. He held three fingers parallel to the table. "Banish the Darkness," he whispered.

"Restore the Light," murmured Cassia.

"I've just cleaned this table over here." He motioned Cassia to a table as if she were the empress herself.

Cassia, however, just stood in front of the bench. "We'd have to send the money to you."

"We're like family." The owner patted the bench. "How could I charge you?"

This time Cassia sat down. "Thank you, Uncle."

Along with Tiny, I sat down on a bench opposite her. "Well, I can tell you that this is one kind of party I don't intend to go to again."

She looked at me as if I were a small child throwing a tantrum. "Well, my family's been giving parties for two generations now. We haven't had much fun so far. But we're going to keep on trying."

I studied her face for a moment. She looked far younger when she was smiling—and yet she was quite serious at the same time. "I can't tell if you're persistent, or just crazy."

"A little of both." Impulsively, she poked me in the arm. "But what if you went to a party and that one *was* fun? Then how would you feel?"

The owner had begun frying something in the kitchen. I could hear the hiss of the oil and smell the delicious aroma that began to fill the wineshop. "Probably still hungry," I said, licking my lips.

She sighed in exasperation. "I thought we were holding a serious discussion. What kind of student are you?"

I threw up my hands. "I'm not at my best when I'm starving." And I could almost feel the rap of Uncle Itchy's bony knuckle on my head, so I added, "Or at most any time."

She leaned her elbows on the table. "Maybe I need a sense of humor, but you could use some confidence in yourself."

The next moment the owner appeared with a huge bowl of noodles and vegetables and a pot of tea. He set them down with a clink and said in a low voice, "We'll get the Manchus next time." He lifted the cups from where they hung on the knob of the teapot lid. "And we'll make sure that those Strangers mind their business when that day comes."

Cassia glanced at Tiny as she took a pair of chopsticks from the owner. She used the same low tone. "What have the Strangers got to do with that?"

The owner regarded her suspiciously. "Why, everything. If they had helped like true children of the T'ang instead of holing up in their villages, we might have won."

I took the other two pairs of chopsticks. "It was lack of cooperation that ruined the party. No one would agree on who was to be in charge."

He looked at me as if I were a fool. I knew that expression well, because my uncle used it on me often enough. "There's talk that they even spied for the Manchus, so they knew all our plans." He nodded to Tiny as I handed him some chopsticks. "What's the matter with your friend? Can't he talk?"

I put my hand warningly on Tiny's wrist. His accent would give his real identity away in a moment, and we'd probably wind up getting kicked out. "No, he can't," I said quickly. "He's been that way since he was born."

"Oh, sorry." The owner dipped his head in apology.

Cassia slipped her chopsticks into the bowl. "Is the Brotherhood putting the blame on the Strangers?"

"Of course." He narrowed his eyes. "I thought you were at Canton?"

"We were," I said, "but we never heard any talk like that. The Brotherhood is just trying to save face."

Cassia kicked me underneath the table. "Now, Brother," she said in an artificially sweet voice, "we were only soldiers. We can't know the whole picture like our uncle here."

I stared at her for a moment. "But—" I tried not to wince as she kicked me again.

"Especially when he's willing to share his wisdom along with his food." Cassia nodded politely to him.

"I guess so," I said lamely, and reached my chopsticks into the bowl. But somehow the noodles didn't taste nearly so good now as they had smelled.

Mollified, the owner scratched his elbow. "Now, I'm a just man, mind you. The Strangers have some real complaints against our kind. We don't always give them a fair deal when it comes to land and rents;

but even so, they shouldn't be getting even by informing on us. We're all in this together."

"We certainly all have to pull together," Cassia agreed. She chatted with the owner for a little while longer until he was satisfied that we had been at Canton, after all.

"Eat hearty, children," he urged us. "I'll be back in the kitchen if you want more." And then he left us.

I leaned forward to whisper, "It sticks in my throat to have to put up with that hogwash."

"You don't seem to be doing so bad," she said, helping herself to a mushroom. "But I know what you mean."

"And you're going to go along with it?" I asked.

"The Brotherhood needs some excuses. Those rumors will die soon enough, and then we can get on with the Work." She glanced at Tiny. "I'm just sorry that you have to put up with that now."

Tiny made a face and patted one shoulder in a long-suffering way as if to indicate that they were broad enough for that burden. "This isn't the first time that this sort of thing has happened," he whispered. "But if you mind your own business, it usually dies down."

Satisfied, Cassia popped the mushroom into her

mouth as she looked at me. "And if you're smart, you won't argue with people."

I squirmed uncomfortably. "But you argue."

"This is for a greater good," Cassia insisted.

"Well," I grunted. "I may not be smart, but I know how to hang around smart people."

Chapter Six

I thought that I might have trouble keeping a conversation going with Cassia; but the rest of that day the talk seemed to flow effortlessly. And it wasn't just teasing her. I quickly found out that that was too easy with someone as deadly serious as she was. I was telling about my scheme for all shopkeepers to give discounts to those who could entertain them when she just shook her head.

"You're just as crazy as Foxfire. He wants to do away with the emperor."

Stunned, I froze in mid stride. That was an even

crazier notion than that a person didn't need a clan. "But who's going to talk to Heaven for the rest of us?"

She shrugged. "I suppose we'll have to do our own talking."

"But if the right emperor is on the throne, then things go right." I struggled clumsily for the correct words. "And if there's a wrong one—like now—then things get bad." It was one of those rare times when I was willing to take the risk of being serious with someone; but I felt like I could talk to her about serious things and she would really listen.

"It sounds crazy to me too," she confessed, "but so did the golden mountain."

I scratched my head. "It's hard to tell what's ridiculous from what's true."

"I know." Cassia folded her arms. "Sometimes I think it's all the demons' doing. They turned the whole world upside down."

With a little jump I landed on my hands and began walking upside down. "Then we'll have to do this." I went on for about five paces before I tumbled to the ground in a small cloud of dust.

"Can't you be serious for more than a moment?" Cassia planted her hands on her hips, but she fought to keep a straight face. Suddenly she just broke down and laughed. "I can't help it. I just can't." Her shoulders began to shake as she laughed, but then I noticed the tears sliding down her cheeks. "This is terrible. Terrible. Father's hardly dead and I'm laughing. And it's all your fault."

Feeling guilty, I looked at Tiny and Tiny just looked back at me. As big and as strong as he was, he was helpless in this situation.

"Sometimes"—I cleared my throat—"sometimes things are beyond tears. All that's left to do then is to laugh. You have to laugh because it hurts so."

"I never heard that," she snuffled.

"My friend Ducky says it all the time," I assured her.

"I suppose he ought to know," Tiny observed. "He'd have a lonely enough life on the road."

Sniffing, Cassia brushed back tears. "I don't know what else to do. Crying doesn't seem to ease the hurt any."

"And laughing does?"

"Some," she admitted.

I was glad that there was something I could do for her after all. "So," I said in a stern, teacherlike voice, "we'll continue your lessons."

It took me the rest of the day, but I managed to

get her to the point where she could at least half tease someone.

The problem with the Strangers was the last thing on our minds when we finally came to a halt. The late-evening sun made our shadows stretch out before us like long streamers of water until our shadows merged with the shadows of the orchard trees. The roofs of a village, sitting on top of its hill, caught the last rays of sunlight.

I yawned. "We'd better find an inn."

Cassia stepped over a cat that had chosen to take a nap in the middle of the road. "Inns cost money."

I rubbed the muscles in my cheek. "Then maybe we could find someone to put you up in a house, and Tiny and I could sleep in a stable."

"Hosts ask questions. They'll want to know why we're so far from home." Crooking a finger at us, she stepped off the road into the orchard.

I tilted my head up to study the village. Smoke from the evening cooking fires began to rise like a bouquet of thin, ghostly flowers. It looked innocent enough, but she was right. People were bound to ask questions, and what if there were informers?

As Tiny and I followed her into the trees, I put a hand up to a branch, but the fruit wasn't ripe yet.

The smell of the cooking fires drifted down to us, so my stomach began to growl. "Down, tiger," I said to it and looked at Cassia's back. "Say, what are we going to do for a meal?"

"I saved a little rice from tea." She patted a lump in the gun bundle as she made her way through the orchard.

"Well," I started to grumble, "I do like some kind of topping, but I've gotten by with less, so—"

Suddenly she motioned me to silence. In the distance I could hear the sound of someone walking over dead leaves. Hurriedly, Cassia squatted down and loosened the bundle. Three large balls of rice dropped into the dirt as she left the cloth loosely covering the gun.

Carefully, I shuffled my feet so that I was standing by a tree to her right, ready to grab the person. I tried to smile at Cassia encouragingly, but she was too busy watching for the walker to notice me.

He was a tall man, so that he sometimes had to bend to make his way among the densely planted trees. He looked to be in his fifties, and his hair was a pepper gray. Over his shoulder was a pole, and at either end was a bundle of kindling and firewood. He halted when he saw us and eyed us warily.

Cassia gave him a forced smile as her hand slipped underneath the cloth. I was sure that her finger was on the trigger. "How've you been eating?" she tried to ask casually.

The man spoke with a Stranger accent. "I get by."

Tiny spoke up then. "You don't mind if my sister and brother sleep under the trees, do you?"

The Stranger seemed surprised at meeting another Stranger in the orchard. He eyed us cautiously. "They're not my trees. Do what you want."

I leaned against a tree trunk. "Folks don't make things too easy for you around here, do they?"

He jerked his head at me. "What's it to you?"

I folded my arms. "I've got another friend who's a Stranger."

He shifted his grip on the pole. "Whereabouts?"

"Up by Phoenix Village." I nodded in the general direction.

"I had a friend who retired up there." The man spread his legs a little more so he could balance his load better. "His name was Ducky."

I tapped my fingertip against my shoulder. "With a scar right here. He got it when he was a boy."

Satisfied that I really knew Ducky, the man smiled. "Yes, I was there when the landlord's cane left that

[75]

mark. Then the landlord made Ducky's father beat him for being insolent. A little after that Ducky ran off with a traveling medicine show."

I picked up a couple of sticks. "He told me he got his scar when he argued about some of the expenses that the landlord was adding on to the rent."

The man heaved a big sigh as he reminisced. "Ducky was always bound to think with his tongue before his mind. So how's he doing in Phoenix Village?"

I began to toss the sticks back and forth between my hands. "His tongue is still likely to get him into trouble."

The man watched me juggle. "Well, for heaven's sake, tell him to keep his mouth shut for a while. Feelings are running high."

I caught first one stick and then the other in my right hand. "We could see that while we were traveling."

The man started on. "And tell him that Yammer told you to warn him."

"I will. And good luck." I waved a good-bye.

Cassia waited until he was gone before she began to rewrap her gun. Yammer didn't realize how close he'd come to dying. "You're a man of some talents."

I strolled over to her and picked up the three rice balls. "My uncle says that it's always for useless things, though." I wiped the rice on my shirt. "The rice has gotten all dirty."

"You said you wanted a topping." She laughed at me. I suppose there were worse people to make an escape with.

We found a place underneath a large tree—the kind that grows the fruit called dragon's eye. I think its growing days were over; but whether through sentiment or because the folks thought there was some magic to it, it had been left alone. It stood like a gnarled giant that dwarfed the surrounding trees.

When we finally sat down, I tried to nurse my rice along. "Things really sound serious."

Cassia began to wolf down her rice as if all the excitement had added an edge to her appetite. "It won't last much longer. People are bound to come to their senses."

Tiny took a worried bite of rice. "I hope so."

It didn't take us long to finish our meager portions of rice. Afterward Cassia stretched and lay down with her bundle cradled in her arms. "Better get some sleep. We've got another long day ahead of us."

Before I could say anything, we heard the angry shout. "There he goes."

I whirled around and looked up the slope. I could just make out the walls of the village through the branches of the upper trees. A torch appeared there and then a dozen more, like a cloud of stars that began to pour down the slope.

Cassia began to unwrap her gun, but I grabbed hold of an overhead branch. "Don't be a fool. You can't stand off a whole village." I pulled myself up into the tree. "It's better to hide."

Cassia hesitated and then stooped, grabbing her bundle and handing it up to me slowly—as if she were reluctant to give that up for even a moment.

I slid backward along the branch toward the trunk. In the meantime Cassia was shinnying up into the tree's large fork as the shouting grew louder. "Tiny, come on."

The big man was scrabbling at the trunk. "I'm afraid I'm not too good at this."

Cassia reached a hand down. "Grab hold."

But I didn't see how she could lift Tiny's bulk up into the tree by herself, so I lay down on the branch and held out my hand as well. "Come on, Tiny."

Desperately, Tiny reached his hand up and caught mine. Cassia slid over to grasp his wrist as well, and together we managed to pull Tiny up into the tree just as a panting man ran beneath us.

His long queue flew out behind him as his feet

crunched the dead leaves. I recognized the Stranger, Yammer. One moment he was running with his fists pumping at the air, and the next moment he was flying through the air and sprawling in the dirt.

He scrambled to his feet almost immediately, and we could see that his face was so contorted by fear that it no longer seemed quite human. His lips were twisted back to reveal his teeth, and his eyelids were drawn up so that his eyes were whiter and wider than a normal human's. He took one step and fell with a grunt.

He rolled over onto his back as he raised one leg and clasped his ankle. He squinted in pain as if he had twisted it on some unseen root. And suddenly the torchlight was bright beneath us as the other villagers surrounded the Stranger.

His eyes opened in terror and he gave a start—as if he saw us hiding in the branches of the tree, but the villagers were too occupied with him to turn around and notice us. I thought for a moment that he might try to save himself by turning us in as spies or something; but he kept silent, though the villagers narrowed the ring around him.

A fat villager waved his torch at the Stranger. "Have you told lies to the Manchus about this village?"

He held a forearm protectively before his face as sparks swirled in the air. "I haven't told anything. I mind my own business."

The fat man waved the torch as a casual threat. "And see that you do. Don't forget who settled this land."

Yammer lowered his arm. "And my people have been here three hundred years."

It was the wrong thing to say. A bamboo stick cracked across his back, knocking him face forward into the dirt. A thin, chinless man rocked up and down on the balls of his feet. "That still doesn't make it yours."

"Just remember your place." A young tough darted in to kick Yammer in the side.

The fat man let that go on for a while, and then he stepped forward and held his torch up importantly. "That's enough. I think he knows better than to carry tales to the Manchus."

The thin man added one last blow to the Stranger's back, but he didn't even grunt in pain. "And don't get uppity with us anymore."

The crowd began to move back toward the village with a self-satisfied air—as if they had just done their civic duty, like building a temple, instead of having beaten up one of their neighbors. They talked and even laughed to one another in a pleased way.

When their voices had diminished to a distant murmur, I risked lowering my head out of the tree and looked at things upside down. The villagers were now distant specks of light, so I let myself drop out of the tree.

"Are you all right?" I whispered to Yammer. When he didn't answer, I crept over to him.

"Is he alive?" Cassia had climbed down from the tree.

I felt for a pulse. It was still there, good and strong. Apparently, he had just fainted from the beating. "Yes. They make his kind very tough." There were bloody streaks on his shirt where the bamboo had broken his skin. "I'd better get some water. There was a stream a little ways down in the valley."

"The village might have patrols against grain thieves," she warned.

"I'll risk it." I took off my shirt. "See what you can do for him in the meantime."

I snuck through the orchard cautiously. The moonlight glimmered on the leafy vegetables in the fields far away. It was such a peaceful scene that it was hard to shake the feeling that I wasn't really awake.

These were ordinary folk who should be tending their plants, not charging about in a mob.

I was just about to step out of the orchard when I saw the silhouette of a spearman. I crouched, but he didn't seem to notice as he paced along in a bored way with his spear resting across his shoulders and his arms draped over the spear shaft.

I waited until he was out of sight and then made my way over to the stream that wandered around the foot of the hill. Holding both ends of my shirt, I lowered it into the water. Then I tried to rush back as fast as I could before all the water trickled through my shirt. I hoped that the guard wasn't very alert, or they could follow the trail all the way back to us.

In the meantime, Yammer had regained consciousness and Cassia had gotten off his shirt—though I could only guess at how much pain that had caused. She was now daubing some kind of salve on his cuts. Though she was doing it as lightly as she could, the Stranger would still start and wince.

I knelt down in front of him and held out my shirt. "I brought some water."

He leaned forward, his hands supporting the wet bottom of the shirt, and he sucked up the water thirstily. There was still a little left when he looked at

Cassia and then at me. "Thank you. Those idiots thought I might settle some old scores by informing on them."

"Is this a rebel village?" Cassia asked doubtfully.

"Heavens, no." Yammer wiped clumsily at his mouth. "But they thought I might make up lies." He gave a little shake of his head. "The funny thing is that I would have sworn that I was getting along fine with them. You just can't tell about those people."

"They're not always that bad." The loyal Tiny felt honor bound to defend us. "They're just afraid, but they can't take it out on the ones they're afraid of— the Manchus. So they pick on a target they can reach."

"Wait till they come for you," Yammer said.

"I'll stay at home," Tiny insisted stubbornly. "They can't be angry at what they can't see."

"I thought they'd ignore me too." Yammer winced when he laughed.

Cassia's face got a determined look, like she was ready to take on an entire army. "Nothing's going to happen in our homes. We'll make sure of that." Cassia nodded confidently to me. "Won't we?"

She seemed so sure that I would agree with her

that all I could do was jerk my head up and down quickly. "Of course."

Yammer's hand shot out, and he grasped my wrist so hard that I lost hold of my wet shirt and it slapped against the ground. "But you may not be enough. Warn Ducky to be careful."

Chapter Seven

We tried to pass through that troubled countryside as fast as we could, but we had to stop for food—whatever we could earn, or get from some house that Cassia knew was safe, or even beg. In all those places we could hear the angry, bitter talk against the Strangers.

And instead of dying in time, the talk only got worse. By the time we neared our homes, the Strangers were getting the blame for a lot more than the war—everything from the price of rice to the bugs that might have invaded a house. It must have been terrible for Tiny, worrying about his wife and child.

Even so, I was still sorry to see the journey end. Cassia might be crabby and high-handed, but she was also tough, bright, and capable. I couldn't think of better company with whom to run away from a horde of bloodthirsty Manchus.

We paused by the stand of spotted bamboo by a fork in the road. The left path wound up the the left side of the valley to Three Willows, her clan's home; and the right led to mine, Phoenix Village.

Tiny broke into a broad grin as he stopped in the middle of the road. "I guess we made it."

I was going to miss the big man and his quiet strength. "It didn't seem likely back at Canton, did it?" I started to nod my head to him, but to my surprise he caught me up in his arms and gave me a big hug.

"This is advice from one outcast to another," he whispered fiercely in my ear. "Face your enemies and never let them know that they've hurt you."

When he let go, I stepped back. His face had its usual quiet expression, but I knew now that it was a mask. There was more to the big man than he let out. "I will."

"It's been nice getting to know you," Cassia said.

I turned to Cassia. To my astonishment, I realized

that I was going to miss her more than I thought. "It's too bad that the trip's over. No one's ever going to take you for a comedian, but at least you can tell a joke sometimes."

She smiled. Somehow smiles came easier to her now, despite everything she had been through—but this one seemed a little sad. "And no one will ever take you for a philosopher, but at least you know that someone can like you for more than a few laughs."

"Yes, that's something." I stood there, watching as they took the fork that I would never and could never take. It was the last time that I would ever see them, and I wanted to fix their images in my memory.

Tiny walked on quickly enough, but Cassia trudged on as if she were carrying a hundred kilos on her back. Suddenly she came to a halt. "No," I could hear her say. "No, I just can't let it happen."

Both surprised and happy, I watched her storm back down the path toward me. "I can't unleash you on the world the way you are."

I plucked a leaf from the bamboo. "And I wanted to get you so you could tell a joke regularly. It's still pretty hit-or-miss."

She folded an arm over her stomach. "And you still try to mug and make faces while you're talking about the most important things. The tutoring is only half finished." I guess she was as reluctant to end things as I was, and that realization gave me this funny feeling—like ants were racing up and down beneath my skin.

I chewed on the leaf. "I can just see what will happen when I come up to the gates of your village and announce to the guard that I'm your joke teacher." In my nervousness, my breath was coming a little too quickly.

She took the leaf away from me in mock exasperation. "Honestly, I can't let you out of my sight. How do you know that leaf wasn't poisonous?" She flung it away. "I can't trust you out of my sight for one moment."

In some ways she was like the big sister that I'd never had. "I guess you can't," I agreed, and added wistfully, "But what are we going to do?" This just seemed to be repeating the pain of separation all over again.

She took a deep breath and let it out slowly, as if she were just about to leap off a mountain. "We could meet someplace else." She nodded to the ridge that separated our two valleys. "My clan has a cemetery at the top. I often visit my mother's grave in the late afternoon."

I thought she was joking at first, but she was perfectly serious. Well, she was always much bolder than me. It really was too good to be true. "I thought there were patrols."

Cassia was speaking quickly now—almost breathlessly. "I suppose I shouldn't be telling an enemy of the clan, but I never saw many while I was there." She pointed at the line of trees that marked the ridge's beginning. "And even if they did come by, they never look very hard. Someone could hide there."

I wished that I could have matched Cassia's boldness, but I didn't like charging blindly into trouble. Everything was just happening too fast for me to sort it out. "People might get the wrong impression if they found out."

I might have known she wasn't afraid of anything. "Let them. I'll joke my people out of their assumptions, and you can out-philosophize yours."

The ants seemed to have gotten into my blood. I could feel them surging up and down my veins so that it was impossible to think. Almost in desperation, I turned to Tiny. He was a steady, levelheaded fellow. "Is that what you think?"

He simply smiled. "If you need a lookout, just ask me."

"You see?" Cassia raised an eyebrow. "It's all set."

I had the feeling that our escape from the Manchus

would be nothing compared to what might happen. But I told myself, Squeaky, my boy, you've been cautious all your life. Be wild for a change. I took a deep breath and then leaped into the dark future. "All right," I said. "It's a deal. Tomorrow afternoon?"

"Yes, at the Hour of the Monkey." She straightened my sleeve affectionately and wagged a finger at me, as if she wanted to play the big sister again. "Stand tall when you go home. Don't let anyone shrink you to a clown. You were the one who tried to save our homeland, and they didn't."

I stayed by the thicket and watched her trudge up the path. She turned at the halfway point and waved at me, and I waved back. I was glad that I wasn't going to lose her company. I turned then and started up the path to my village. A few steps and the ridge hid her from view.

But I'd see her tomorrow. Feeling easier inside, I strode up the path to my home.

Everything seemed so much smaller as I stepped into the valley. The little fields looked like broken pieces of brown-and-green tile that someone had scattered over the valley floor. And up on one wall of the valley the village, with its tiled roofs peeking over the dirty walls, looked like some child's toy.

Heads swiveled as I made my way over the dikes,

which doubled both as boundaries between the fields and as paths. "Hey, Squeaky, where've you been?" a cousin called.

I caught the joke at the tip of my tongue. I was the new, dignified Squeaky, after all. So I just turned and fixed him with a stern look. "Making the world safe for you." It was Melon Head.

"Or cleaner." He nodded to my dirty clothes. "It looks more like you were just trying to dust it."

I tried to think of what Cassia would have done. The old way would have been to agree with him and maybe tell a few jokes at my own expense, but I refused. "At the moment, there's more important things on my mind." I added, "I'll leave the dirt to you."

People in the nearby fields laughed, and Melon Head stared up at me in a hurt, puzzled way. And I was sorry for a moment, because he wasn't a bad fellow. He even tried to make the best of it. "I've got plenty of dirt to share."

I would have liked to oblige him and clown with him for a bit—maybe even get down into the dirt and sling it about—but I could feel the clan watching me intently. And anyway, I was beginning to feel pretty tired and hungry. "Some other time." I shrugged. "Is my uncle around?" I surveyed the valley floor, but I didn't see him.

A disappointed Melon Head went back to his fields. "No, I think his rheumatism is bothering him."

I paused on the path that zigzagged up the side of the valley wall to the village. All around me were the terraced fields of sandier soil where people would grow sweet potatoes.

Above me the guard at the gates was leaning against a gatepost and scratching his belly. A pig snored at his feet. And suddenly I realized why the valley and the village itself seemed so much smaller. It hadn't changed at all. I had. I'd been to Canton—or at least I had seen the buildings behind the walls. And after that, Phoenix Village no longer seemed like the center of the universe.

It made me feel suddenly very sad and small, because I knew I could never really go home again. As I trudged up the path, I wanted nothing better than to go into my uncle's house and crawl onto my mat and go to sleep and just forget about how I felt. But suddenly the guard lowered his spear to bar my way. "And who are you?"

The old Squeaky would have gone along with the joke and maybe gotten down on his knees and begged to be allowed in, but I just wasn't in the mood anymore. Instead, I caught hold of the spear shaft and swept my leg around in the way I had been taught at camp. I caught the guard in the back of the knee and sent him falling.

"Hey," he protested as I jerked the spear out of his hand. He fell on top of the pig, who woke with an angry squeal. It was hard to say who was more startled—the guard or the pig. But it was safe to say that neither of them liked it much. The man struggled to get to his feet, but unfortunately the squirming pig kept bumping his arms, so he kept sprawling over it.

"Maybe you'll remember the next time I pass by." With a satisfied air, I twirled the spear one-handed until the blade was pointed at the ground, and I jabbed it hard into the dirt. Maybe there really was something to what Cassia had said. When I turned around, I saw that some of the clan had come out into the streets to see the commotion.

I waited for them to greet me, but they just stared— as if I were indeed some wanderer who had come into the village. I began to make my way down the narrow, winding street to my uncle's house. It was a strange feeling to pass by houses that I had known all my life and yet that seemed to have shrunk, or to see people whom I had known since I was a boy and have them simply watch me walk by with cautious, wondering eyes.

I was beginning to feel like I had wandered into

the wrong village by the time I reached Uncle Itchy's house. Wondering if Cassia and Tiny were thinking the same thing, I swung the gates open, and that motion made a slight breeze that suddenly swept along all the medicinal leaves that had been drying on a mat in the little courtyard. Many of them rose into the air and settled into a tub of water.

With an angry little screech, Uncle Itchy jumped to his feet, but paused when he saw it was me. "You."

I hardly remembered my parents because they had died when I was five. In the time since then, Uncle Itchy had been both mother and father to me. "I came back, Uncle."

Uncle Itchy's face was a study. He seemed to want to both smile with relief and scowl at the same time. But as the proverb goes, "Praise makes for bent children, the stick for upright ones." Uncle could never let me know how worried he had been about me, or it might spoil me.

Instead, he charged toward me, his long, thick queue bouncing like a heavy rope on his back. "Leave it to you to come home at the worst possible moment."

Uncle Itchy had been grabbing my ear ever since I was orphaned at five, and he didn't see any reason to stop even when I had grown two heads taller than him. His hand shot upward to seize that particular portion of my body and—as was part of my habit—I leaned forward obligingly. It was a wonder that my earlobes didn't reach down to my knees with all the stretching Uncle Itchy gave them.

For all of the rheumatism in his knees, Uncle Itchy could move his legs well enough. He hopped up and down on one leg while he used the other to kick me in the rear. "Run off right before the harvest so I have to give even more of it away to hire help. And then I try to raise a little cash by selling some herbs, and you come back and ruin them."

Despite what Cassia had said about standing tall, I'm afraid I forgot everything when I was with Uncle Itchy. "Yes, Uncle," I mumbled frantically. "I'm sorry, Uncle." And I said other such things just as if I were a small boy of five and not a "warrior" of nineteen.

In the meantime the people who had been in the streets had gathered by the open gates. Some were laughing at the spectacle while others were calling for more people to come and see. I didn't doubt that by this afternoon the story would be all over the village: how Uncle Itchy had shrunk my big britches for me. I had thought that Cassia's tutoring might make a difference, but I'd been mistaken as I'd been so many times before. Little Squeaky Lau, the clown of Phoenix Village, had come home.

Chapter Eight

I should say in Uncle Itchy's defense that he promptly took me into the house and fed me—though he did lead me in by my ear. He set down a whole bowl of vegetables in front of me and a big bowl of steaming rice and then sat down opposite me, his toes just touching the floor.

I noticed only one rice bowl. "Aren't you going to eat, Uncle?"

He folded his arms. "Later. I already had a little snack."

And at the sight of more food than I'd seen in

months, I began to eat. It was almost all gone before I started to look around my old house. It was just as I had left it—a bare little one-room house with sooty walls and an old stove, black with years of fires. And then I saw the empty baskets near it. Apparently, Uncle Itchy hadn't been doing too well while I'd been gone.

I set the bowl down, ashamed. "What are you going to eat, Uncle?"

He waved his hand for me to continue. "Oh, I'll find something. It's more important to fatten you up a little. People will think that you forgot to eat while you were away."

I laid my chopsticks across the mouth of the bowl. It was like Uncle Itchy to disguise a kindness with a mild insult. "I've had enough."

"You're sure?"

I used a fingertip to slide the bowl a little closer to him. "Please."

"Well, if you're full." Uncle took the bowl and chopsticks and began to wolf the food down. With the bowl still in his hand, he followed me out into the courtyard. Though Uncle Itchy would rather have died than admitted it, he'd missed me.

I told him everything about my travels—omitting Tiny, Cassia, and her father. I didn't know how it would sit with Uncle to have been helped by a Young, whom he regarded as much an enemy as the Manchus.

To be honest, I didn't have much to say. The most action I had seen had been during my escape with Cassia and her father. So instead I described the villages in the delta land near Canton, where the houses had been two stories high because of the flooding there. And I went on to talk about the rebel camp, where there had been so many peddlers and camp followers and storytellers that it had seemed more like a fair than a military establishment.

Still, I think what I had to say was more important than the village gossip—certainly more vital than hearing about how the Widow tried to entice other people's ducks into her yard so that they could lay their eggs there. But you wouldn't have known it from the way Uncle Itchy talked. He made it sound as if rescuing Cousin Melon Head's black pig from a ditch was as important as overthrowing the Manchus. And I guess in his mind it was.

And before I'd left our village, I guess that kind of talk had been just as important to me, but not now. "And how's Ducky?" I finally asked. "I didn't see him in the valley."

Uncle Itchy began scratching the back of his neck furiously, like a dog chasing down a pesky flea. His scratching had gotten him his nickname. "Holed up in his house, and if you have any sense, that's where you'll leave him. This is one situation where you won't be able to help him with jokes and clowning."

I'd helped Ducky when I was younger. When the other children began to pick on him, I could usually distract them by my clowning. But from Uncle Itchy's warning, it sounded as if that poisonous gossip about the Strangers had spread to Phoenix Village. "What's been happening while I've been gone?"

Uncle Itchy switched to rubbing his neck. "He's just learning not to be so pushy anymore. He doesn't have any right to work the best fields."

I hated to risk a quarrel with Uncle Itchy, but I couldn't let that statement stand. "That's up to his landlords. They want the best tenant for their fields."

He flung a handful of wet leaves down on a mat. "Now just hold on a moment. This is our valley. This is our ancestors' land, and don't you forget it."

"He's been in the village for ten years. Doesn't that count for something?"

"And our clan's been here for at least twenty generations, and maybe more. That will always make him a Stranger."

"I think I understand a little bit about that now," I said quietly.

Uncle Itchy looked down and spread the leaves out on the mat. "Well, maybe you do, boy. You've seen a bit more of the world than your Uncle Itchy now. But just remember this." He looked up sharply. "When times are bad and the tiger's at the door, you can really only trust your own kind."

"I only have one enemy and that's the Manchus," I said, and stumped out of the courtyard.

"Leave it to you to pick impossible friends" was Uncle Itchy's parting shot.

Outside, I paused as people looked at me with open curiosity. Aware of their eyes, I squared my shoulders and deliberately crossed the street to Ducky's.

For a moment I just stared at the gates and walls. Ducky had always tried to keep them clean, but they were spattered now with filth. Picking out a clean spot, I knocked on the gates, and when there wasn't any answer, I caught hold of the top of one gate and pulled myself up. "Hey, Ducky. It's me, Squeaky."

Knowing that I couldn't hang there indefinitely, I pulled myself over the gates and dropped into the courtyard. The large threshing basket had been smashed, and several mats had been torn. But the worst thing of all was that someone had taken a knife and slashed crossing lines over Ducky's door.

When I was small, the door was the wonder of the neighborhood. With bright red paint Ducky had painted various scenes from his wanderings, and he had traveled far—from the palaces of Peking to the stones of the Great Wall. Looking at Ducky's door had been like looking at the Middle Kingdom in miniature, and now some vandals had defaced it.

"Ducky?"

The door creaked open a fraction and I saw an eyeball. "It really is you." The door swung wide and Ducky stood there. He was a short man in his late fifties. The pleasant smile on his face contrasted with the meat cleaver in his hand.

I patted my ribs. "Go ahead and take a cut, but you're not going to get much except bones."

Ducky stepped into the courtyard with that peculiar shuffle that was almost a waddle. "You'd taste terrible anyway after all that camp food." But his face was crinkled up in a big smile of welcome. I could always count on Ducky to be glad to see me.

"Things have been bad?" I nudged the broken basket with my toe.

"It happened while I was in the fields. They didn't have the guts to do it while I was home. They even marked my poor door." His pliant face put on a woeful expression. A conversation with Ducky was sometimes like talking to an entire village. "I couldn't tell whether it was critics or farmers."

"Do you think it was . . . ?" I pointed a finger to my right, where Lumpy had his house. The village bully lost no love for Ducky.

"I think so," Ducky whispered, "but I don't have any proof."

I picked my way through the wreckage. "I'm sorry, Ducky."

Ducky pressed his lips together, closed his eyes, and gave his head a little shake as if it were no big thing. "I've had audiences try to do worse. But I'll just have to make the best of it." He swung his cleaver toward his house. "If you don't mind the poor housekeeping, come in for some tea."

There was even more wreckage in Ducky's house. His table and benches had been smashed, and what hadn't been broken had been torn. He got a fire going in his big square stove. "You'll have to forgive the smell. I tried to clean the stove the best I could, but I still can't quite get the aroma of urine out of it."

I stood beside a bench that Ducky seemed to be mending with scrap wood. "That's nothing compared to camp."

"And this old acrobat wants to hear all about it."

Ducky checked outside before he closed the door. I noticed that he left his cleaver right by the doorway, where it would be easy to grab. "I've always wanted to play the big time, and there you were—right in the center of the stage."

I could always trust that old acrobat to make me feel important. Even when I was a boy, he always took the time to listen as attentively as he would have to a man.

"We—" I corrected myself quickly. "I mean, *I* met Yammer."

"That's a name from the past." He cleaned a cup with the bottom of his shirt. "I haven't seen him since I was a boy. How is he?"

"Bad." I quickly told him about the beating.

"Catch." Ducky tossed the cup to me and I caught it. He tossed another cup to me, and I almost missed that one.

"It's a good thing that you caught that one. Those are the only two unbroken ones left." The water had started to bubble on the stove and he returned to it.

I stared at Ducky as he stood by his stove. "You're taking the vandalism a lot better than I did."

Ducky returned my stare. "It's the first time that we've ever talked about this sort of thing, but it wouldn't be the first time that this kind of thing has happened."

And I was suddenly aware of the gulf between us that I had never thought about before. "I'm sorry."

Ducky didn't have a face that was meant for frowns. His face broke into his broad, familiar grin. "I don't blame you." He flung a pinch of tea into a mended teapot and poured water into it. "But you said 'we met Yammer.' "

"I met someone." I juggled the cups experimentally; and then, remembering that Ducky couldn't afford to have me break them, I set them down on the ground.

"Wait, wait. If you're going to tell this story right, make sure your audience is seated." Ducky brought the teapot over to the center of the room and set it down. "Now you can begin," he said, plopping down.

So over tea, I told him all about my adventures— and this time I included Tiny, Cassia, and the Gallant.

"You mean they really were Youngs from over the ridge?" Ducky took a sip of his tea.

"She didn't trust me at first, but I won her over," I said smugly.

Ducky, however, didn't seemed thrilled by my new friends. "War does make funny allies." He studied me over the rim of his teacup. "Or is it more than that?"

"No, of course not. She's just like a big sister." I

held my cup just beneath my chin, feeling the steaming tea rise about my face. "We're going to try to get together when we can." I added hastily, "Just to talk, mind you."

Ducky crouched over and put on his best imitation of Uncle Itchy's scowl. "Friends with a Young," he mused. "The next thing you know, you'll be wanting to marry an elephant."

I sprawled out my legs. "Think of all the work that she could do in the fields."

"Yes, but you'd have to build a bigger house." He set down his cup, and he put on his stern school-teacher expression. "But take some advice from someone who knows about trouble. Don't let it go beyond this."

I refused to back down though. "You're sitting in what looks like the middle of a battlefield, and you're telling me all this?"

Ducky puffed out his chest and, arching his fingers like the legs of a spider, pressed the tips just below his throat. It was a perfect imitation of my cousin Lumpy, who always looked as if he were trying to pose for his own monument. "I'd have to face it wherever I went. I'd rather choose where I have to fight." He flung a hand out toward the ridge. "But she isn't necessary."

Part of me knew that he was being reasonable, but the other part felt stubborn. And I was a little surprised at that. I'd made a whole life out of avoiding fights, but maybe Cassia was having some effect on me after all. "That I have to see."

Ducky seemed genuinely surprised that I didn't take his advice right away. Pursing his lips thoughtfully, he pulled at his chin. "You have changed." With a sigh he picked up his teacup again. "But I don't know if it's for better or for . . . worse."

Chapter Nine

Cassia was waiting up at the cemetery just as she had said she would. She was picking the weeds from a grave as if her own life depended on it. She glanced at me as I came up. "My mother's," she said by way of explanation.

I sat down next to her. "How was your homecoming?"

"A lot of questions about my father." She held a handful of weeds away from her. "But they didn't get a whole lot of answers." Bits of dirt pattered down, sounding like raindrops. "Still, they've been expecting my family to die violent deaths." She waved the weeds at me. "And you?"

I got up for a moment and picked up the rock that I'd sat on. Something had upset her. Her words came a bit too quickly, and her eyes darted all around as if she were restless. "Some think that I've changed," I said carefully, "and some don't."

She teased her chin with the weed tops. "And don't they think you're a big hero of the Work?"

I chucked the rock over my shoulder. "Me? I think that they still consider me a clown—but one with suicidal impulses now."

She flung the weeds away as if she wished she could throw away something else with them. "At least they're not trying to marry you off."

I wondered if that was what was bothering her. For some reason I felt as if someone had suddenly emptied out my insides so that I was all hollow. If I hadn't known any better, I would have said that I was jealous. I covered up my dismay by drawing a knee against my chest and cupping my hands around it. "No, but then I don't have a brother sitting on a mountain of gold."

Her hand shot out and she gripped my wrist with a fierce strength. "There are other ways of becoming a big man in a village."

I looked down in surprise at her hand. "Well, I don't think that's going to be any problem with me."

Embarrassed, she let go. "It's just that the clan wouldn't take my brother seriously either until he went over and started sending money home." She turned her palm up and sadly curled her fingers closed. "In the end, it's always money and property that counts with a clan."

I laced my fingers together. "First rice. Then honor."

She plucked a blade of grass. "I think it's that sentiment that really killed my father." She used the grass like a spear and jabbed it at the air. "Maybe I'll have that put on his tablet."

"For your home?" I asked cautiously. Perhaps her clan's attitude was upsetting her.

"Uncle Blacky—he's the village scholar—is writing it out on a nice piece of wood, and then we'll have it carved out and gilded in the city." She tried to snap the blade of grass in two, but it simply bent. "It's the best I can do since I couldn't bring Father home."

I placed my hands behind me and leaned back. I could try to give her what comfort I could. "I didn't know your father for very long, but I think he'd understand."

In sheer frustration, Cassia threw the grass blade

from her. "I wish he were here now. He could set some sense into the clan."

Suddenly I knew what was getting at her. "About the Strangers?"

Startled, she slapped her hands on her knees. "You too?"

"They wrecked my friend's house." I tilted forward. "What happened to Tiny's family while he was gone?"

She wrapped her arms around herself as if she felt a sudden chill. "Just words and insults. His wife, Aster, is small like me, but fierce."

"Fiercer than you?" I couldn't help being skeptical.

She raised one palm and swept it back and forth as if erasing something. "In a different way. No one wins an argument with Aster. She can take someone apart and have everyone laughing while she does it."

I rubbed the dirt from one palm. "Well, between Tiny and her, they ought to be safe enough."

"I don't know." She gripped her trouser leg. "I've helped them so that they own their own fields now. I didn't realize that there was so much resentment in the village until now." She raised her hands and pressed them beneath her throat. "I'm sure some of it is against me, too."

"You see? No one resents a clown." I held up my hands. "Why do you want me to change?"

She pointed at me. "No one resents the clown—except the clown himself."

I had to admit that she sometimes knew how to hit the target. "All right, all right. But the real problem is what to do about our clans' stupidities."

"Well—" Suddenly her head lifted. "There must be some kind of fire in your village."

I twisted around to see the ugly black column of smoke rising upward. I jumped to my feet. I remember feeling very annoyed. It wasn't bad enough that the province was at war and that our two clans were feuding; but just when we were starting to feel close, something like this had to happen. "I'd better see what's wrong."

"We ought to finish our conversation sometime," she called after me.

I backed slowly through the cemetery. "Then let's meet tomorrow at the same time. Maybe we won't be interrupted again."

"Yes, I'd like that." She stood up as if she were worried. "And be careful in the meantime."

Nodding to her, I pivoted and began to run back toward Phoenix Village.

It was Ducky's house that was on fire. One gate still hung burning on its hinges while the other had crashed a little to the side. I raced through the burning gateway into the courtyard. Ducky had taken off his shirt and was flapping it at the burning window frame. He turned when he heard me come in. "Someone put a burning straw man against my gates, but the wind blew sparks onto the house."

By now the roof was half hidden by fire. "Never mind the fire." A swirl of smoke curled down around us, and I coughed for a moment. "I'd save what I could of your seeds."

Ducky looked back at the house. "But I went hungry just so I could buy the paint to fix up the house."

Outside, though, we could hear Lumpy bellowing in his loud voice, "Form a bucket brigade. Bucket brigade."

I felt proud of the clan at that moment. Faced with the same common trouble, they could forget about their petty feuds and jealousies.

He gave a little half shuffle to stare out into the street, where people were lining up between the village well and his house. He blinked his eyes as if he couldn't quite believe it. "They're really going to help."

"They can feel ashamed of themselves," I said quietly.

Ducky smiled suddenly, so he seemed more like his old self. "I guess I am going to need seed to plant."

"And food to eat." Holding an arm up in front of my face, I dashed through the burning doorway. Flames licked at my sides and then I was stumbling inside. Bright light came from the fire overhead; but even so, it was hard to see things for the smoke inside.

Coughing, Ducky stumbled against me. "Over there." He took my shoulder and turned me to see several large baskets.

I grabbed one basket while Ducky tried to pile two on top of one another. "Ducky, use your head," I shouted. "We'll try to come back."

Ducky stubbornly tried to haul both baskets across the floor. "And if we don't?"

I lifted the heavy basket with a grunt. "You're the one who's always telling me to make the best of it." I staggered past him. "You can't do that if you're not alive." The flames seemed to fill the doorway now, and I hesitated.

"It's not very nice to have your own sage advice thrown back at you," he said from behind me. "But

I must be a smart person if you're quoting me. Let's go."

I pressed my face against the basket and, taking a breath, rushed forward. I felt sudden pain on my arms and hands, but in a moment I was stumbling outside.

"You're on fire!" I heard Uncle Itchy yell.

Chapter Ten

I dumped the basket on the ground and saw that my sleeves had caught fire. I stared at them stupidly, thinking that they looked like the bright, transparent petals of some crystal flower.

"Down, you idiots." Uncle Itchy tripped me and I fell forward.

"Hey," Ducky shouted, and I heard him fall a moment later, rice seed spilling as he dropped his basket.

But Uncle Itchy wasn't about to apologize. "Roll in the dirt." I felt his strong, small hands forcing me back and forth, and I finally got the idea. I began to roll in the dirt of Ducky's courtyard, and through the dust and smoke I could see Uncle Itchy forcing Ducky to do the same.

The dirt stung against my skin and I sat up. The flames all seemed to be out, but I could feel a pain across my back; and when I looked down at my arms, they were raw and bleeding with blackened edges. "Are you all right?" a worried Uncle Itchy asked.

"Ducky?" I tried to look past him.

Uncle Itchy craned his neck to look at my back after he had looked at my arms. "His burns are no worse than yours. They'll smart for a few weeks, but you'll be all right." Once he was sure that I was okay, he showed his relief by scolding me. "But you ought to be spending plenty of sleepless nights trying to find a comfortable position and thinking about what a fool you are."

By that time Lumpy had the bucket brigade formed, and he had climbed up on the wall at the corner where Ducky's wall met his on the left. Lumpy thrust out his arms to balance himself, and once he was steady, he squatted down. "Up here."

Someone raised a bucket to him, and, taking it in both hands, he rose carefully. And then, with equal care, he flung the water onto the roof of the next house. He tossed the bucket down behind him, where someone must have caught it, because I didn't hear it land. "Somebody get water on the other house. We've got to keep them wet."

I stared up at him, not quite believing what I had heard. The clan was worried about protecting the other houses—not about helping Ducky.

"Hey, what about Ducky's?" I shouted up to Lumpy.

"It's gone," he said. In the meantime Cousin Boxy had gotten up on the opposite corner to fling water on the other house.

Ducky jumped to his feet angrily and rushed over to Lumpy. "You wouldn't be saying that if I was one of your clan."

Lumpy squatted down to take the next bucket. He might have been right about Ducky's house being lost, but he didn't pick the most diplomatic way of putting it. "No one asked you to stay on."

Ducky grabbed Lumpy's shirt. "Some of your clan started this fire."

Lumpy put one hand down on the wall to balance himself while he shook free from Ducky. "And we'll assign the blame later." He turned to take a large pan of water.

"Save my house, damn you!" Ducky seized Lumpy's ankle in both his hands.

Lumpy squatted there awkwardly as he tried not to spill the heavy pan. "I told you that we can't."

"Damn you! Damn you all!" With a sudden jerk, Ducky pulled Lumpy's leg out from under him, and with a yell, Lumpy tumbled forward. Water drenched the two of them as they lay for a moment in the courtyard, and then Lumpy rose with a splutter.

"You're crazy," he said as he sat up.

Ducky scrambled to all fours and tried to rise, but slipped on the now-muddy patch in his courtyard. "All of you make me crazy."

I started to go over to get between the two of them; but Uncle Itchy caught my arm. "Stay out of this, boy."

He didn't have that strong a hold on me—probably because he was afraid of hurting my burned arm. In fact, a pigeon could have pulled free from his light grip. I thought of all of Cassia's fine speeches about how we would prevent just such stupidity. I hadn't disagreed with her. It was time to back up words with actions.

Of all the times to do the brave thing, it was now. But to tell the truth, as ashamed as I was of the clan, I was also a little frightened of them. They were really all that I knew; and after my short stay in the cold, harsh world outside our valley, I wasn't about to defy them. So, Heaven help me, I stayed where I was. But I couldn't help thinking about what the Gallant had said about the Light being in each of us. I felt like I'd failed him, too. As the fire burned so brightly in front of me, I felt like the sootiest of shadows.

The only thing I did was to shout to Ducky. "Don't be a fool, Ducky."

Lumpy got up on one knee and reached his hand underneath his shirt to the waistband of his pants. "You stay away from me."

"You've tormented me long enough." Ducky lunged for him and got his hands around Lumpy's throat.

Lumpy pulled something bright and metallic from his pants. The object caught the light for a moment, so I couldn't see what it was. Then he turned it slightly, and I could see the blade of a knife. "You're crazy," he shouted. His eyes were wide and staring in his face, and his whole body was rigid with fright.

"You can't do this. You can't," Ducky yelled.

"Ducky, get away," I shouted, but it was too late.

Lumpy's arm jerked upward and the knife went in with a sick sound. Ducky gasped and his mouth stayed open. He rolled his eyes not toward Lumpy but toward me. The two of them stayed frozen for what seemed a long time.

"Ducky." I pulled free from Uncle Itchy this time and ran toward him.

"The show's finished," he murmured, and then it was as if someone had broken the sticks to a shadow puppet. He just seemed to pitch sideways toward me.

I dropped to my knees and caught him. Lumpy slid away on one knee. "You saw it. He attacked me."

"You drove him to it," I said.

"I was trying to save the village." Lumpy rose slowly.

"You could have understood his feelings," Uncle Itchy snapped. "But no, you had to carry on that silly argument of yours."

"You can't reason with a crazy man." Lumpy said it more for the benefit of the others than for us.

"You killed him."

Lumpy became aware of the blood on his hand. He wiped it hastily on the wall. "I didn't know what I was doing."

"You killed him," I insisted. But in my heart I knew it was as much my fault as it was his. I was the coward. I was the murderer.

"No, I just meant to scare him." Lumpy began to back toward the gates.

"You and your silly feud." I flung a handful of dirt at him.

The other gate crashed to the ground in a burst of sparks. "No, no," Lumpy cried, and whirling around, he ran over the burning gate and out into the street.

I looked back at Ducky and then lowered him to the ground. "Why couldn't you make the best of things, like you always did?"

But I already knew the answer. You can only do that for so long before you start to wear thin inside. Cassia would have called it pride. Whatever it was, it was something that I didn't think I had—not after the way I had let Ducky down.

Uncle Itchy touched my shoulder. "Come along, boy. We'll bury him later."

I could hear water splashing, and I looked up to see that someone else had taken Lumpy's place on the wall. The clan certainly protected its own. "He deserved better than this, Uncle."

Uncle Itchy sighed. "I never said that he was a bad fellow. He just happened to not be one of us."

"And what does that make us?" I demanded, and

for once it was Uncle Itchy who dropped his eyes first.

I stared at Uncle Itchy in silence until a little old woman slipped into the courtyard. Behind her were a half dozen others who picked their way past the burning gates. In their arms they had large bowls. "What are you doing?"

"He took this from us," the first one quavered. She knelt beside the spilled rice seed. "It's our valley, after all."

"His corpse isn't even cold and you're already gathering like vultures." I hadn't known that I could get any angrier, but I was.

She scooped a handful of seed up and dumped it into her basket as another woman dropped to her knees next to her. "He doesn't need this." She slapped in annoyance at the second woman's hands. "This is mine."

The second one jerked back. "There's plenty for all."

In the meantime one of the others had jerked the lid off the second seed basket and begun filling her bowl. Immediately, three others began to jostle and argue with one another as they tried to put their bowls in too.

"Don't be harsh on them, boy," Uncle Itchy whispered. "They're hungry and frightened—and people do funny things then."

"But why do they have to be hungry and frightened?" I asked angrily.

"Some people start feuds; other people steal." Uncle Itchy dipped his head a little bit. "Other people tell jokes." He meant me, of course.

But he was wrong now. "The jokes just died with Ducky," I said quietly. "And so did the clown."

Chapter Eleven

The next day the only thing that kept me going was that I was going to get to see Cassia. Of all the people in the area, I felt as if she alone would understand my grief. Uncle Itchy was feeling uncomfortable about what had happened, but he wasn't about to condemn the clan. "I'm not saying they had an excuse for what happened, but they did have their reasons. Things just got out of hand."

I stared at him across the table. "They should never have been allowed to go that far."

Uncle Itchy rubbed the back of his neck. "When

you're young, it's so easy to say what's right and what's wrong—"

"All I know is that my friend's dead." I could still smell the acrid smoke rising from the site of Ducky's house.

Uncle began to dig his nails into his skin. "Accusations aren't going to bring him back."

I spread out my hands in front of me. "But I just feel so . . . so angry."

Again it was Uncle who looked away. "All right. All right. We're all murderers and arsonists, and we'll never be anything else." He was really scratching now. "Just do me a favor and keep your opinions to yourself."

"But—" I began to protest.

"You owe me that much for taking you in." Uncle Itchy slapped his hand against the table. "Oh, I know that your father would have done a better job, but I've tried to do my best. At least you never starved. And I've never asked you to work any harder than me."

It was my turn to glance away uncomfortably. "Do you know that this is the first time that we've ever talked about my adoption?"

"Of course we have." Uncle sounded so positive. "Plenty of times."

Without looking up, I swiped my hand across the table top to clean away some rice grains. "No, Uncle," I said just as firmly. "This is the first time. I know— because I've tried a lot of times before, but you always put me off. You never talk about it with anyone."

"I've never been one to parade my charity like other folk." He began to scratch again, but in a slower, puzzled way, like someone who has wandered into unknown territory.

I looked up sharply. "Why did you adopt me? Because you felt sorry for me?"

He rocked back, startled. "Heaven help you, no, boy. I wanted you. You were so much like my little brother when he was small. And you were so little and helpless and trusting." He picked up a small jar of ointment from the table. "I always wanted children, boy, but it just never worked out for me."

I watched him concentrate on lifting the jar lid. "Are you . . . are you very disappointed by the results?"

Uncle began to slowly smear the ointment over the back of his neck where he had scratched. "No, boy. It could have been worse." Since Uncle downplayed everything, it meant that he was actually pleased.

I couldn't help thinking of the hundreds of clumsy little kindnesses Uncle would do me—in his offhand way as if it were only an afterthought—even when we both knew it wasn't: the piece of candy he brought back from a trip to town or the toy laboriously made out of straw. "Well, I do owe you a lot," I admitted.

He clapped the lid on the jar once again. "For both our sakes, put last night behind you."

If I did what Uncle asked, I would feel like even more of a coward—as if I had deserted Ducky twice. But Ducky was dead now; and besides, I shouldn't blame Uncle for my own acts of cowardice.

I sighed. "All right. I'll keep quiet, but," I warned him, "I'm not forgetting."

Uncle Itchy wiped his hand on his shirt. "I suppose that's as much as anyone can ask."

I got up. "Will you let me use the shovel? Ducky ought to be buried."

Uncle hesitated and then rose from his bench. "I'll do more than that. I'll help you."

I jerked a thumb toward outside. "And the clan?"

Uncle thrust out his chin. "They can think what they like of an act of charity." Uncle did have his good points, after all.

We buried Ducky in a corner of the clan cemetery, which lay at the rear of the valley in rocky soil surrounded by pine trees. We had wrapped a mat around the body, but it was obvious what we were carrying.

Still, no one looked our way—as if they all wanted to forget last night.

The rest of the day seemed to drag on until it was time to meet Cassia again. I worked with Uncle in the fields until the late afternoon. Then I made an excuse about going for a walk, and Uncle didn't argue.

I told myself that Ducky was going to be my last failure. I couldn't live the rest of my life clowning and making empty promises. I'd tell Cassia everything.

Cassia was waiting for me once again by her mother's grave; but to my disappointment, there was a baby on her lap and next to her was a small, round-faced woman. Behind them was Tiny. I was surprised at how much I'd been counting on talking to her alone.

Before I could say anything, the woman threw back her head and let out a long wail in exaggerated sadness. "Ai-i-i-i-yah!" And rolling her eyes, she began to croon,

> *"I stubbed my toe on a stone;*
> *I scolded the stone*
> *—Blame for you I had none."*

She had the accent of a Stranger.

Cassia nudged the woman with her elbow. "Shush. Your wailing's set off the baby."

The woman dismissed the baby airily. "Oh, let him exercise his lungs. It's good for him." But she did lean over to make soothing nonsense sounds to him.

In the meantime Cassia had begun to jiggle him on her knee. "That's the stupidest song I've ever heard. I suppose she won't get mad until he sets her hair on fire."

The woman straightened. "I always figured that a man wrote that song, anyway." She glanced slyly behind her at Tiny.

"But this had to be written by a woman." Cassia inclined her head toward the woman and began in a soft, pleasant soprano,

> *"If this is how it is,*
> *Then let it be so,*
> *For even the greatest love*
> *At last has to go."*

It must have been a familiar routine, because the woman touched her head against Cassia's and joined in.

> *"The petals have to fall*
> *From the reddest flower,*
> *And wine, though it's old and sweet,*
> *In the end turns sour."*

After talk like that, I wasn't sure whether to step into the cemetery or not; but the woman had turned when she straightened up, and she saw me.

"Whoops." She nudged Cassia. "Is that him?"

Feeling as if I were caught, I stepped into the cemetery—even though I wasn't prepared for this much company. "How've you been eating, Tiny?"

The big man grinned broadly as if he were glad to see me, but he simply said, "I get by."

The woman elbowed Tiny in the stomach. "Listen to that big fool. You'd think I didn't slave over a stove making him four meals a day."

Tiny took a cautious step back as he rubbed his stomach. "Have you been following my advice?"

I don't know if he would have said I'd really faced the enemy and not let them see the pain. I hadn't done much of anything. I winced as I felt all my earlier resolve draining away from me. "I've been trying."

Cassia had been smiling until she saw my face change. "What happened yesterday?"

I slowed as I picked my way through the cemetery. I had been so eager to complain to Cassia about the others that I hadn't given any thought to what she might think about me. Would she condemn me for holding back? I wasn't sure that I could stand it if she despised me. "They killed Ducky," I blurted out.

Cassia handed the baby to the woman. "He was the Stranger," she explained.

"They're trying to claim that it was an accident," I added quickly.

The woman cradled the baby as if her arms were enough to protect it. "It's these crazy times."

"There have been some ugly scenes in Three Willows too." Cassia patted the baby sympathetically.

"I hope there was nothing serious." I sat down on a small mound of dirt.

"It'll take more than a few fools to chase us out." The woman had begun to twist slowly back and forth from the waist. Despite myself, I was beginning to like the woman. She was not only funny, but she was tough as well.

Cassia nodded to the woman. "This is my friend, Aster, and Otter, her son."

I remembered one of the times that Tiny had talked about his family. "Then you're Tiny's wife," I said to Aster.

The baby had calmed down by now and was busy wriggling in Aster's arms. I supposed that was why they had nicknamed him Otter. "Otter was curious about you." Aster wrestled with the noisy baby. "So he insisted I take him along with his Auntie Cassia."

I raised one knee and clasped my hands over it. "This isn't the best time to meet."

To my surprise, Cassia reached her hand out shyly toward me. "Sometimes I think you and I are the only two sane people in the province besides Tiny and Aster."

I just looked at her hand guiltily. If she had really known what I had done, she wouldn't be saying such things to me. "They thought Ducky was uppity, but he was just trying to earn a living like the rest of us."

"That's right. We're just supposed to take their leavings," Aster muttered.

Cassia's hand faltered in the air and then dropped. She seemed a little embarrassed and puzzled because I didn't take it. "What happened?"

I wanted to confess my cowardice to her. But I was afraid of what she would say. She could be a very stern judge, and I realized that I didn't want to lose her friendship. It would have been like losing the last window when I was locked away in a prison cell. So instead I changed the story around. "I did what I could, but he got stabbed before I could do anything."

"Of course you did." She gripped my shoulder warmly. "That's why we have to talk out against this insanity. So it doesn't happen again."

Her words just cut even deeper into me. I'd come here to share my troubles with her, and instead I was living out a lie. Once a clown, always a clown. "There's small chance of that in my village. Ducky was the only Stranger, and I doubt if any more would try to come in."

Her hand tightened. She had a surprisingly strong grip. "Well, there are three in my village, and I intend to see that nothing happens to them."

She had such courage that I was ashamed to be with her. If Cassia had been there last night, Ducky wouldn't have died. She was such a sharp contrast to me. I jerked my head at Aster. "Maybe you ought to think about leaving for a while until folks cool down."

But Aster was just as brave as her friend. "This is my home. But even if we were going to run away, where would we go? Tiny says the whole province has gone crazy."

I leaned forward, desperately wanting to save Aster and her family, at least. "You could go up to that new city the British demons are building to the north. They call it Hong Kong; and I hear they rule by their own laws, so the feud wouldn't mean anything."

Aster smiled with one corner of her mouth. "That's irony for you. We have to go to the British demons for protection from our own kind."

"No, we won't," Tiny said with quiet dignity. "This is our home. We're not going to be driven away."

Cassia wasn't about to back down either. "You won't." She let go of me and rested her hand on the gun, which she had leaned against a stone. "We'll keep order here—even if I have to use this."

Chapter Twelve

It was easy for Cassia to talk about keeping order; but not so easy to do. It was about all I could do to get to see her.

First of all, Uncle gave me a funny look when I told him I was going for a short walk. "Again?"

I wasn't about to back down on this at least. "I've got a lot to think about, Uncle."

Uncle gave a guilty hitch to his pants. "I wish you'd forget about Ducky."

"I wish I could too." I headed out of the fields, and Uncle didn't say anything.

But I had an even bigger problem waiting for me on the ridgetop near the cemetery. Lumpy had taken it in his head to patrol more—as if hordes of avenging Strangers were about to descend on our village at any moment.

"What are you doing here?" he demanded.

I clasped my hands behind my back and tried to look as innocent as I could. "Are you planning something for me, too?"

He ground the butt of his spear against the ground like some opera general. "Things got out of hand with Ducky. We just wanted to scare him." He jerked his head at me. "You of all people should understand. You know how the Strangers sabotaged the rebellion. They say that the Strangers are carrying tales now to the Manchus just so the Strangers can get revenge."

I should have kept my mouth shut and concentrated on getting away from Lumpy; but I guess Cassia's tutoring was having some effect, because I couldn't help saying, "Well, you did a good job of scaring Ducky. You scared him to death."

Lumpy straightened. "It was an accident, I tell you. An accident."

"It was a very convenient one." And pivoting my heel, I turned and walked back into our valley and then up the opposite slope. It took a while to work my way along the ridgetop there as I made my way back to the cemetery.

Cassia was by herself this time. She was busy pacing up and down. "I didn't think you were coming."

I almost told her about Lumpy, but then I wondered if she might think it was too dangerous to go on meeting. I knew I didn't want to stop, so I just made myself smile like the old Squeaky. "I had some family business to handle." It was true in a way, since Lumpy and I belonged to the same clan.

"Your uncle?" She sat down on a large rock.

I sat down on a rock next to her. "Cousins."

She picked at the green lichen that covered one side of her rock. "The only time people come to me is to borrow money or ask a favor."

I crossed my right leg over my left. "And what did they ask for before you were rich?"

She stared at some of the crumbled lichen in her hand. "They just never came by. I was the serpent's child, after all."

I wagged my right foot up and down. "You look perfectly normal to me."

Her fingers closed over the lichen. "It was a long time ago that an ancestor of my mother married a serpent spirit, so I suppose there's more human blood in me than serpent now." She rested the fist in her lap. "But they said I was just too strange to be human. They thought I was cold and sharp just like a serpent would be."

I hid my own guilt by fussing with my cuff. I'd thought just the same things about her when we'd first met. "You can be almost relentlessly logical when it comes to the Work."

"If we all were, our country would be free now." And her face began to take on that tight, cold look it had when she was getting ready to defend the Work.

I stilled my foot as I tried to change the subject. "Well, what do they say about you now that you're rich?"

She opened her fist and began to brush the green stains from her palm. "They still think I'm strange—only they don't say it out loud anymore."

She was within a half meter of me, but at that moment she looked far away—back when she was an isolated little girl. Even if I hugged Cassia at that moment, there would be no way to reach that sad child. "You must have been terribly lonely."

When it came to protecting herself, there was no one quite as quick as Cassia—whether it was with her fists or with her inner defenses. Her mouth pressed itself into a tight line. "I don't want you to feel sorry for me."

I could have teased her out of her mood; there wasn't anybody I couldn't get to laugh for me. But this friendship ought to be different somehow. For a change, I'd try to be honest. "I know how you felt, that's all." I waited, feeling a little scared that she might go storming off.

But Cassia just studied me like I was some rare, exotic flower that she'd just found. "I guess you do."

I dropped my foot to the ground. "You're not mad?"

She drew her head back. "Why do you think I'd get angry at the truth?"

"I don't know." It was my turn to be edgy. "I guess I'm always afraid that people will do that if they know what I really feel."

"And I'm always afraid that people will scold me for not being serious and honest." She brushed her fingertips across my wrist and then shyly snatched her hand back. "We're two of a kind, after all."

I thought that over for a moment and then nodded my head. "I suppose we are. Behind that somber face you're all a-bubble with laughter and smiles."

She laughed, and it was a good sound. "Yes, and behind that clown face, you're full of scowls and frowns."

I wrinkled my forehead and pretended to think. "And I ponder things like why is there dust."

She gave me a good-natured poke. "And to think I almost took off your head the first time we met."

"There are worse ways to meet."

She pressed a fingertip against her lips for a moment. "That's true. The second time we met, I nearly slit your throat and then I actually dumped you into a pit of manure."

I laughed at that, and she seemed pleased. "You see. Things have been definitely getting better." And I knew that there was nothing that was going to keep me from seeing her.

And the rest of the afternoon was spent teasing one another lightly, as if the Strangers and Lumpy and everyone else were far away.

I wasn't supposed to meet her until three days later, but the next day we got word of a village only some ten kilometers away where the village militia had beaten up the Strangers there. And Lumpy was announcing to one and all that the Strangers probably had it coming.

Well, maybe I wasn't about to defy a whole village like I'm sure Cassia would, but I could take Lumpy down a peg or two.

"Oh," I said, "and what should we do now that you've killed off our only Stranger? Go out and rent some to beat up?"

The others started to laugh a little guiltily until Lumpy shouted them down. Then he jabbed a finger at me. "You're asking for trouble unless you change your attitude."

"It's easier to change my pants than my attitude," I said breezily, and got the others to laughing again. I'd always used jokes to get along with people, but now I was finding that it could be a weapon in an argument.

"The Strangers . . ." Lumpy began, but then paused while he waited for the laughter to end. "The Strangers are the biggest threat right now to the peace of this district."

I cupped a hand behind my ear and bent forward as if I were straining to hear. "I don't hear any of them shouting in the middle of the village. If you ask me, you're the biggest threat."

"Well, no one asked—" he began to say when I pretended to fall backward as if the force of his voice had knocked me over.

It was easy to begin clowning then with the rest of the crowd, but this time I had a purpose. They were so busy laughing that Lumpy never got to finish his rabble-rousing speech. It was a dangerous game to play, with him standing there and getting redder and redder in the face while he clutched at his spear—

in a way it was like tweaking the tail of a tiger every time it tried to roar. But I was having my revenge for Ducky. And I was sure that the clan would stop Lumpy before he tried to do anything.

But that day when I went out for a walk, Lumpy followed me. I took my time strolling around the valley—always in sight of the clan, and eventually he got bored and left me alone. And the next day he didn't even try, so when it was the day to see Cassia I felt safe enough.

Cassia was all full of indignation about the beatings when I did see her. "And my clan is being so self-righteous about the news." She added smugly, "But I set them straight."

My own little triumph now seemed small in comparison to what she had done. I made my way through the cemetery over to her. "Did you argue with them, or did you try joking this time?"

"Arguing, of course." She took my hand—the way a beginning swimmer likes to grip a rope or a tree root for security. "I thought you, of all people, would understand."

Hastily, I stroked the back of her fingers the way I would try to soothe an angry cat. The last thing I wanted was to quarrel with my only friend. "I just meant that sometimes when you keep blowing on a fire, you only fan it higher instead of putting it out."

"So far they've listened," she shot back.

My hand stilled. She was obviously getting annoyed with me, but I had to go on—for her sake if not for mine. "You're rich. And your brother is sitting on a mountain of gold," I pointed out. "When their men go overseas, they probably look to him for help. They're not about to jeopardize that by crossing you."

Irritated, she drew her hand back. "Then I'm safe enough."

I was sorry to lose that contact with her, but I was determined to save her from trouble. "For now. Your clan may be wrong about the Strangers, but that doesn't make their feelings any weaker. You can only hit them over the head so long."

She shook her head. "It's not my way to stand by when I see a wrong happening."

That accusation cut deep inside me. "I'm not asking you to, but you can try teasing them out of that mood."

"That's not my way." She tilted up her chin defiantly.

"Well, your way is going to lead to a fight," I warned.

"I'm ready."

It wasn't any use arguing with her. I sighed in

exasperation. "Now I know how you got so good at fighting. You had to. You're so pigheaded that you must always be getting into fights."

She gave my arm a little frustrated shake. "You're still worried about pleasing everyone. But don't you see? When you do that, you please everyone but yourself."

"But I'm not like you. You're so . . ." I fumbled for the right word.

She arched an eyebrow. "Serious?"

"Well, yes; but you're also . . ."

"Pushy?" she suggested.

"That too." I wagged my finger as I found the word for which I'd been searching. "You're just so self-contained. Like some strong, fine wine that's been sealed into a jar."

"Then how do you know what's really in the jar?" she asked playfully.

"I read the label," I tossed back.

She gave a snort. "Then don't go into town. Those hucksters will take away every bit of cash from you." She hugged herself. "Anyway, I'm not sure that I want to be called a dusty old jar."

"I didn't say you were that." I held up my hand. "Sometimes I feel like an old cracked cup that won't hold anything." I raised and lowered one shoulder. "There's really nothing to me."

She mimicked me by raising and lowering her shoulder. "Listen to me. You can't go by what other people say." She tapped her fingers against her heart. "You have to go by what's in here."

I cocked my head to the side. "But what do you see in me?"

She leaned her head to one side like a small, inquisitive bird. "Someone who doesn't like himself very much." She added, "But someone who should."

"You must like lost causes."

"Difficult ones," she corrected me, and then patted my arm affectionately. "Well, I'm not asking you to help me. Just don't get in my way when the fighting starts."

I dragged my foot back slowly through the dirt. "You're not afraid?"

"Of course I am. But my mother"—she motioned to the grave—"and my father never backed away from a fight in their lives, and neither will I."

While I admired her courage, I wasn't nearly so confident as she was about the future. "I suppose it wouldn't do any good to tell you to be careful."

"No," she agreed, "it wouldn't."

During the next few months, the madness only seemed to spread and the incidents seemed to increase. It was as if one beating caused twelve more. By the summer the whole province seemed ready to explode again—not against the Manchus, but against our own neighbors.

I had more run-ins with Lumpy, but my clowning always got me out of trouble until the day he decided to follow me right when I was supposed to see Cassia. "I'm just going for a walk." I waved to him. "Can't we talk later?"

"Maybe I want to go for a walk and see the sights you see," he said.

I would have been safe enough if I'd dodged around him and gotten back into my village, but I'd made a promise to myself that nothing was going to stop me from meeting Cassia. I might fail in everything else in this life, but it was one promise I intended to keep. So I started to run up the slope. I heard him blunder after me. When I passed the rhododendron bush, I darted around and broke into a run, diving into a small gully whose mouth was hidden by other shrubs. I'd noticed it on one of my other walks and made a note to myself to use it on some occasion like this. What I hadn't seen before this was that it was full of brambles. The thorns tore at my skin and my clothes, but I made myself ignore the pain while he charged on past.

I was feeling pretty good about myself as I made my way back to the cemetery. Cassia was already there pacing up and down as if she were worried about something.

I tried to run to her, but a scrape on my knee bothered me so that I could only manage a limp. "What's wrong? Are you in trouble?"

"You're the trouble." She paused in mid step with her back still to me. "You've never been this late before."

I tried to pass it all off as a joke, since I didn't want to worry her about Lumpy. Only this was one time when it was the wrong thing to do. "Trouble is my specialty. It comes in six different colors and five assorted sizes."

"I was beginning to think you were dead in some ditch. And now you just come strolling in and making a joke—" She rounded on her heel, but the indignant expression on her face changed to horror when she looked in my direction.

"What is it?" I whirled around to look behind me. I half expected to see Lumpy standing there, but there was no one.

"What happened?" Cassia plucked at my torn shirt.

"You look like you've been dragged through a bush."

I'd been in such a hurry to get here that I looked down at myself for the first time. My shirt and pants were ripped from the brambles, and my skin had been cut in a half dozen places and the dirt and sweat had mixed together into muddy streaks. I wiped at one of them. "More or less. I had to get away from my cousin Lumpy."

She fingered one of the tears regretfully. "If I had my needle, I could fix your shirt."

I wiped my hands on my pants, but that didn't get my palms much cleaner. "My uncle's used to the sight. I was always coming home roughed up when I was a child."

"Why was Lumpy after you?" Cassia took my arm as if I were sixty and started to lead me over to the spot where we usually sat.

I didn't want to scare Cassia, so I just said, "We haven't exactly gotten along since Ducky died."

But Cassia guessed this time. "He's starting to get suspicious, isn't he?"

"I'm afraid so." It finally began to sink in that Cassia had been pacing originally because she was worried about me. It made me feel both strangely happy and sad at the same time. I'd never thought I'd ever have anyone care for me besides Uncle and Ducky, and

[148]

yet Cassia did. And right when I had discovered that, it sounded as if we were going to have to stop seeing one another.

When we sat down, she kept her hand on my arm. "I ought to tell you not to meet me anymore."

It was strange, but my stomach started to twist like the time when Red Legs had come charging up the dock. I thought I knew what she was going to say next, and I wanted to head her off. "I think that's my decision. Not yours."

"No, it's mine too." Her voice tightened, and she almost bit off the words as if each one were hurting her to admit. "Try to understand. I didn't want to let anyone else get close to me. The few people I let do that just seem to leave me alone. First it was my mother. Then my brother. And then my father."

"And I'm not going to leave you," I broke in quickly. I cupped my hand desperately over hers—as if I were standing on a ledge and about to fall into some bottomless pit. "I don't know if I'll be able to see you as often, but I will see you. I swear."

She stared at me coldly, levelly—as if over the sights of a gun. "Let me finish."

I felt as if the ledge on which I was standing were suddenly narrowing. "No." I shook my head. "I know it's hard to take the word of a clown and a fool. But

I really mean this. I feel different with you." I was a little surprised at that—like I hadn't been willing to admit that to myself. "I feel good. And I'm not about to give that up."

"Are you done?" She arched one eyebrow.

I dipped my head cautiously. "For the moment." I felt myself tensing inside like a climber getting ready to claw for any hand- or foothold that he could get.

Her hand tightened on my arm. "What I was going to say before you interrupted was that I didn't want to let anyone get close to me. But somehow you did."

Despite everything, I felt a little thrill. "Should I apologize?"

But Cassia simply ignored me as she often did when she was arguing some fine point of the Work. "I should tell you not to risk coming anymore." Her voice dropped in sudden misery. "But I can't." And she looked at her mother's grave as if she were begging her mother to understand.

I would have given a whoop and done a dance right there if I wasn't in front of her mother's grave. "But this is wonderful. I—"

Suddenly she clamped a hand over my mouth. She didn't look at me but studied the surrounding pine trees. "The birds have gone quiet." She took her gun, which was leaning against a sapling.

I nodded my head and followed her as she slid low over the ground into some bushes near her mother's grave. I could feel her body, pressing warmly against me as much for comfort as for the narrow space. It was three armed men who tramped through the cemetery.

Cassia's breath tickled my ear as she whispered. "It's a patrol from my village."

We huddled there until they had stomped away. "Well," Cassia said, "they're gone." Still, she didn't move.

I leaned my head against hers. "Good."

"I must be part serpent." Cassia sounded just as miserable as before now that the danger was past. "Anyone with common sense would stop right now."

"Then I must be part serpent too," I said, and tightened the arm that I had around her waist.

She shoved me away almost savagely. "This is crazy. I don't have time for a boyfriend. I have the Work." Gun in hand, she scrambled away from me and didn't stop until she was in the middle of the cemetery.

I got to my feet more slowly. "What did I do wrong?"

She straightened her clothes. "It's not you. It's me." She began to walk toward her village, but pivoted. "I'll see you in five days?"

I straightened my shirt. "If that's what you want."

"Yes, believe it or not." She disappeared abruptly down the slope.

I went for walks for the next four days. Once Lumpy followed me, but I managed to lose him again. I was a little pleased and surprised at myself. I didn't think that I'd ever be this determined to do anything. When I saw Cassia the next time, she was back to her old big-sisterly self.

We kept to that same pattern after that. I would still go for a short stroll almost every day, but I would go to see Cassia only every two days or so. Sometimes Lumpy would trail me, but I always managed to ditch him whether I was going to see Cassia or not. If he had brought in help, I might have a harder time, but he was too proud to admit to anyone that I could best him in anything. I suppose I shouldn't have done it, but I couldn't help rubbing it in sometimes. I'd wait by the village gates with a cup of tea for him when he came back all hot and dusty from looking for me.

And even when I did get together with Cassia, it wasn't all sweetness and light. It seemed like every time we got together, she had some new complaint about how her clan was treating Tiny's family. Finally it got so that I was anxious about her own safety. "Maybe Tiny ought to think about taking his family away someplace. Maybe Hong Kong."

But before she could answer, the birds suddenly went quiet. She grabbed her gun and then she picked up a small jar by her feet.

I nodded my head and followed her to the spot we had used as a hiding place last time. She squirmed in close to me and I felt her drape her arm around my waist, so I did the same to her.

However, it wasn't a patrol from her clan, but from mine. Except they weren't really patrolling. Lumpy led a half dozen swaggering men to the edge of the cemetery, where they stood and waited tensely. The others had spears and hoes, but Lumpy had his special spear.

A moment later we could hear people approaching from the Young side of the valley. Their feet crushed the dead pine needles with crisp, cracking sounds and a half dozen men stepped out. They halted a few meters from us; and a young man with a wispy mustache stepped out. Though some of the whiskers were very long, there was a patch missing above one part of his upper lip—as if a moth had been eating it.

"The fellow with the mustache is Stony," Cassia whispered to me. "He heads up the militia now."

"And Lumpy is the man with the spear," I replied in a low voice. "He heads up our clan's militia. I wonder what they're doing together."

"Thank you for coming," Stony said with a slight bow.

Lumpy leaned on his spear. "You said it would be of interest to us."

Stony pulled at one tip of his mustache. "We just wanted to tell you that if you see our militia massing, it's not against you but against a common enemy."

Lumpy straightened. "The Strangers?"

The young man nodded. "It's time we disciplined them. They've had their own way too long."

Cassia was going to jump out of the bushes, but I wrestled her back to the ground. "Let's hear their plans," I breathed into her ear, and I was grateful when she grew still.

Lumpy cocked his head to one side. "How do we know that this isn't some trick?"

Stony waved a hand. "Man your walls tonight if that'll make you feel easier. But we won't be coming over the ridge."

Lumpy considered that for a moment and then looked at the others. They nodded their heads, and he turned back to the young man. "I think we'll be at our walls anyway tonight. So don't get any ideas about fighting anyone outside your village."

"One enemy at a time." Stony held up his hands.

He gestured to the others, and they disappeared among the pine trees.

With a cautious look over his shoulder, Lumpy motioned our clansmen back toward our village. I lay there for a long while. Somehow in the excitement I'd lost my breath, and it took a moment for me to get it back. "But how were they going to get past you and your gun?"

Cassia rolled over on her side so she could face me directly. "Maybe some of the women were going to distract me." She sniffed. "But they'll be in for a surprise."

I became aware of the fact that I still had my arm around her. "Well, you've got to get your friends away. Take them to the demon city."

Her eyes glanced down at my arm, but she didn't ask me to take it away. "And if they won't go?" She added by way of explanation, "Aster can be even more stubborn than me."

"Make them."

She gave me a shy hug. "Then we'll have our old group together again."

Suddenly I realized that she thought that I would help escort them to Hong Kong. Well, Squeaky, I told myself, it's time to keep some of those promises to yourself. You weren't going to be a coward again. The problem was that I was petrified—of mobs, of wandering in strange territory, of leaving home.

I pointed out to myself that Cassia was counting on me, and I went on arguing with myself; but I couldn't escape the one fact: I was scared. I didn't want to get involved in that madness that was war all over again. As much as it might hurt Cassia and me, I just couldn't do it. It was the same old Squeaky disease all over again. "You know," I warned, "I'm not as brave as you are."

She nudged me with her head. "But you did all right when we were getting away from Canton."

Reluctantly I let go of her. "I didn't have any choice."

She gave me a puzzled look. "And when you do?"

I was paying now for all those other lies and half-truths. Cassia had been the one person whose respect I wanted, but now she was going to see that Squeaky the warrior was Squeaky the clown and coward. But I just couldn't help it. "I can't," I blurted out. "I just can't."

Cassia took in a little sharp breath. "I see." I waited for the lecture, but Cassia was only looking at me sadly—the way some bird in flight might watch a bird with a broken wing. "We'll be all right."

I bit my lip. "I'm sorry."

"You can't help what you are." She handed the jar to me. "Here. This is an ointment for your uncle. My mother always swore by it when someone had to soothe an itchy spot."

I clutched the jar in my hands. "How will I explain this?"

"That's your problem." Rising from the bush, she darted away.

"Be careful," I shouted after her, but she was already gone. And I had the terrible feeling that I would never see her alive again.

Chapter Thirteen

That night I mustered with Uncle Itchy and the rest of our clan's militia, and we marched to the walls. But I made sure that we were near Lumpy during our watch. The day had been hot; and even though the sun had set, the air had stayed so warm and humid that the night just seemed to suck the energy out of everyone.

"How much longer do we have to do this nonsense?" Uncle Itchy grumbled to Lumpy.

"Till the sentries bring us word." Lumpy glanced anxiously at the sky, where the clouds hid the moon.

"Though I don't know if they'll be able to see anything in this weather."

Uncle Itchy sat down on the ledge behind the rampart. "Well, I don't mind telling you that this weather isn't doing my rheumatism any good. I think it's going to rain soon."

Lumpy leaned his back against the wall and propped his elbows on the top. "My bunions say you're wrong."

Uncle Itchy massaged his bad leg. "I'll match my leg to your bunions any time."

Lumpy raised one foot and began to massage it. "What will we bet?"

Suddenly we heard the explosive bang from the ridgetop. Uncle Itchy sat back up so fast that he banged his head against the parapet. "What was that?"

It was hollowed out by the distance, but I knew that sound. "It's a gun."

I jumped to my feet and looked up from the wall. It was hard to make anything out on that cloudy night, but I thought I could see the dark blot of the ridge. Had they made their escape, or had they been caught and trapped?

Others were standing and one of them pointed. "I thought I saw a flash over there."

All thought of bunions vanished from Lumpy's mind

as he straightened up. "All right. Everyone keep a watch out. You never know about these Youngs."

Men adjusted their grips on their spears and waited tensely, studying the darkness for some sign of attack. I think I was the only one who wished that the Youngs were really going to attack us; at least that would mean they were going to leave Cassia and her friends alone.

Someone came crashing through the terraced fields on the slope. "It's me! It's me!"

With an oath, Lumpy laid his spear on top of the wall and cupped his hands around his mouth to amplify his voice. "And who's that, you idiot?"

"Melon Head," came this excited voice. He stepped into the area lit by torchlight. "There's commotion over in Three Willows. They caught the Strangers trying to sneak out."

Lumpy leaned his belly against the wall. "And the clan shot them?"

"No, no, that's just it." Melon Head looked around at all the clan, swelled with the importance of his news. "There was a girl defending them with a gun."

Lumpy turned to Uncle Itchy. "It must be that one they say is part snake demon."

I couldn't hold back any longer. "Did they get away?"

"No, they were driven back into the village." Melon Head pointed.

Something wet touched my cheek and I looked up. Small drops fell in my face. "It's sprinkling."

"That changes things for that snake girl," Lumpy said smugly. "Her powder will be wet now."

"She doesn't have a matchlock," I protested. When Uncle Itchy looked at me sharply, I added weakly, "Or so I hear."

Lumpy tapped his fingers on the rampart. "She'll still use powder, and getting it wet won't help."

"Well, that settles it." Uncle Itchy started away from the wall. "I'm for home." He added over his shoulder, "And next time listen to my leg."

I followed Uncle Itchy from the wall, feeling lower and lower—worse than when I had stood by and let Ducky die. I was going to let her down just like I had Ducky.

It wasn't so much the fighting that I was afraid of—though I didn't welcome it either. It was the idea of leaving the only home I knew and going off to Three Willows. And what if my clan found out somehow? They thought it was bad enough that I'd been friends with a Stranger. What if they knew I'd befriended one of our hereditary enemies?

But I thought of Cassia and Tiny out there somewhere, trying to hold off an angry mob with just a useless gun for protection. And I knew I couldn't live with myself if I just sat safe inside my own little home. Even if they did survive, the guilt would eat away at me until I was all empty inside. No, I wasn't going to hold back this time.

But before I could speak, Uncle Itchy was tugging at my sleeve. "All right, boy. We're out of earshot of the wall. Do you mind telling me why you're moping along and dragging your heels like I was taking you to a spanking?"

We were near our house by then. I jerked my head toward it. "I think we'd better talk inside."

Uncle Itchy raised his eyebrows. "That bad?"

But I pushed past him and opened the gates. With a wary glance at me, he slipped on past me into the house. As soon as I got through the door, he slammed the door shut.

"All right. Tell me what's bothering you," he demanded. I heard him throw his hoe into a corner.

"There's a friend who's in trouble right now," I said, trying to see him in the darkness.

He struck a flint against a stone, making small

bright sparks and a sound that made my skin feel itchy enough to crawl away from my bones. "Do I know him?"

"Her. It's a girl, Uncle." I blinked my eyes as he lit a piece of rice straw.

"I didn't think it was a frog," he snapped. He lit the wick that floated in a little bowl of oil.

"You might be happier if it was," I said. "She's a Young."

Uncle opened and shut his eyes several times and then shook the straw disbelievingly. "Say that again."

"During the uprising, I met a girl from Three Willows. I like her and she likes me."

He jabbed the blackened straw in the direction of Three Willows. "Do you realize what the Youngs have done to us for all these centuries?"

"I think the Youngs have a list of wrongs too." I had a makeshift spear manufactured by tying a kitchen knife to a pole. I began to untie the knife from the pole now. If I was going to go looking for Cassia, I had to travel light.

Uncle plopped down on a bench. It took him a moment to find his breath. "Congratulations, my boy. You've managed to top my worst fears. I used to worry that you might run off with an acrobat or an animal trainer. I should have known you'd do worse than that." His lip curled up scornfully. "A Young?"

"She saved my life, Uncle." I set the knife and pole on the table.

"Yes, yes." He pressed his eyes shut as if he were in pain. "I'm sure she did a lot of nice things for you. Just give me a moment to take all of this in." Uncle used the straw to count on his fingers. "Let's see. She's a Young." The straw lingered over the second fingertip. "And you seem to know a lot about that gun that belongs to that snake of a girl."

I swallowed. "She's not a snake, Uncle."

The straw snapped between Uncle's fingers as he gaped at me. "Merciful heavens. Your friend's not even human."

I squared my shoulders stubbornly. "Those are just rumors, Uncle."

Uncle Itchy began to scratch his shoulder. "You recognize the tree by the leaf."

"I know her, Uncle, and you don't." I tensed, waiting for him to pull at my ear.

But Uncle seemed more surprised than afraid. "And they say magical serpents can take any form they want."

"I'm finally starting to think for myself." I got the

[164]

jar from the shelf, where I had left it. "She sent an ointment for your scratching. It's one of her remedies."

He took the jar from me, handling it as if it were about to explode. "You're hopeless. Heaven knows what magic she put into this."

"It's just a simple herbal cure." I started for the door. "I've talked long enough, Uncle. It's time for me to go."

"Wait, don't go." Uncle Itchy set the jar down on the table.

I looked down at him apologetically. "Don't think I'm ungrateful, Uncle; but this is one time I can't obey you."

He grasped my arm as if he were about to fall. "She means that much to you?"

"I can't let you hold me back again, Uncle." My eyes pleaded silently for understanding. "Not this time."

"You'd give up everything for her?" Uncle demanded.

"If I have to."

He eyed me intently. "Even though she may not be human?"

"Especially if she isn't. She can't count on anyone

[165]

but me and her Stranger friends." I took one last look around at the house that had been my home for so long.

I thought Uncle Itchy would start to storm at me or even kick me again, but he just stepped back and tilted his head as if he were surveying some tower that he had just finished building. "Well, I've been waiting for you to show some real backbone."

"Pardon?" I blinked once.

He seemed both sad and proud at the same time. "You've changed direction more often than a leaf in the wind, boy. Even when you ran off, it seemed more like a lark than because you were serious about the . . . the Work."

"I guess it was," I admitted.

He took a deep breath and then sighed. "And . . . it can get exasperating—especially if you don't have much patience, like me."

"I'm sorry, Uncle." I pried his fingers loose.

His hands hovered for a moment, and then he wagged it at me. "No, no." He sighed. "It was my fault. I was always bossing you around." He swept his arm in an arc. "Oh, I know what people said about me: that I was a little tyrant. But I just . . . just"—he clenched his hand suddenly into a fist—"just wanted to protect you."

"You can't protect me anymore, Uncle." I picked up the knife.

His eyes followed the motion of my hand. "You don't resent what I did?"

"You tried your best. Maybe you just tried too hard." I tucked the knife into my waistband.

Uncle adjusted the position of the knife in my waistband. "If you feel that way, I'll cover for you."

"What?"

He frowned in his usual way when I was being slow, but he didn't scold me. Instead, he forced himself to use a calm, slow tone. "Assuming that they're alive and that you find them, you're going to stay with them for a bit. And people will ask questions here. I'll tell them that you're sick and can't come out. That's one advantage of the feud. No one from here knows what goes on in Three Willows."

"Then you understand why I have to go?"

"No, not really." He pinched my earlobe teasingly. "But I forgive you."

Suddenly I couldn't resist the impulse, and I threw my arms around him. "I don't know if I'll ever see you again, Uncle."

He surprised me by the fierce hug he gave back. "I just hope she has more sense than you do." He shoved me away as if he were irritated with me for making him show that much emotion.

There were two wet spots on the front of my shirt, and I realized that they had been made by his tears. He was crying. "I'm sorry, Uncle. I've tried to be what you wanted."

"Oh, go on." He gave me a hard shove toward the door. Such a little man and such fierce strength.

Chapter Fourteen

I paused among the dark trees looking down on the Youngs' village. For a moment I felt like a fish that looks from the sea onto the land.

And then I saw the lights bobbing in the street outside the spot where Cassia had said was her house. They hovered like a cloud of angry mosquitoes. So I wasn't too late, after all.

"Squeaky, is that you?" I turned to see a puzzled Lumpy and Melon Head hiding behind a tree some ten meters away. Lumpy and Melon Head still had their spears. "I thought you were going home with your uncle. What are you doing here?"

I had to think quickly. This was certainly going to

home with your uncle. What are you doing here?"

I had to think quickly. This was certainly going to complicate my plans. "I . . . I thought I'd go out and do some scouting of my own."

"Just like me." Lumpy thumped the butt of his spear approvingly against the ground. "That rebellion did change you after all, Squeaky."

I banged a heel against the dirt. "All I needed was to get away from home for a little while."

"Well, save yourself the trouble." Lumpy waved for me to join him. "I came up to check. Her clan has her trapped inside a house. I suppose it's hers." He rose. "Come on. Our work's done. Let's have a drink together and talk."

It was strange. All I'd ever wanted as a boy was really to be accepted by the others; and now with Lumpy's friendship, I would gain a respect that all my clowning and joking could never earn me. However, that meant I had to go with him instead of to Cassia.

But maybe I could get away from him, sneak into Cassia's village, and sneak back out. "I still think I'd better look around."

He jerked his spear at me. "I'm the captain of the militia, and I say it isn't necessary."

I'm afraid I hesitated for a moment. Once I started

down the slope, there would be no going back. I would be leaving more than a home; I would be leaving a way of life. Until the war, the clan had been the only world I'd known. It was that time with Ducky all over again—only Cassia's life was at stake now. "We'd better be sure," I said feebly, and took a step toward the bushes.

"I like your spirit, but she's finished down there." Lumpy started toward me. "We might as well go home."

So there it was. I had to make a choice. And suddenly it was as if someone had splashed water on a dirty mirror so that my image stood out sharp and clear. I'd still rather be a clanless man than a soulless man. "Sorry, I've waited long enough." I tried to run, but the drizzle had given the ground a thin covering of slippery mud, so I skidded instead.

"Halt," Lumpy shouted.

Strange, but I felt as if I were suddenly more than naked—as if I'd shed not only my clothes but my bones and skin as well; and relieved of that load, my heart seemed to float down the slope. "You can't order me around anymore, Lumpy."

"Stop him, Melon Head. He was spying for them all this time."

I started to trot down the slope through the orchard

toward the ridgetop and Young territory. Poor Uncle. He wouldn't be able to alibi me out of this situation.

A spear suddenly thudded into the dirt within a meter of me. I slowed and glanced over my shoulder. Melon Head was standing there looking shocked at Lumpy, so I guessed that Lumpy must have thrown it.

My big cousin was standing there shaking his now-empty fists at me. "I'll kill you if you ever set foot in our valley again."

No, I guess this was one mess that all the joking in the world wouldn't get me out of.

I stopped and wrapped my fingers around the shaft of the spear. It was made of some heavy, hard wood. I'd wanted to travel light, but Lumpy had made me change my mind. After all, when someone presents you with a magnificent gift like that, you don't refuse.

"Thank you," I shouted defiantly. I pulled the spear from the dirt as Lumpy went livid with rage.

"You're a dead man, Squeaky," he shouted. "A dead man."

There was no going back now, so taking a deep breath, I plunged down the slope. My momentum carried me forward recklessly through the dead leaves on the ground. I must have made enough noise for a charging elephant. I kept thinking that if I tripped over some unseen root, I would break an ankle for sure. But I couldn't stop.

It was strange to enter the Youngs' territory. The last time I'd done it, I'd been surrounded by the rest of my clan militia when Dusty led us on a raid of their crops. Lumpy had called it a raid that would even up some old scores.

The walls stood some three meters high, but there wasn't anyone on the walls or in the watchtower. I suppose everyone was being entertained by Cassia. The gates themselves were open, as if the mob had charged out and then chased them back into the village.

I'm afraid that my knees began to wobble at the threshold. Up to that point, I could still have gone back. As yet, no one from Cassia's clan had seen me. I could return and maybe claim to be overzealous. But once I entered that street and began fighting, I would be more alone than I could ever imagine—a person without a clan. I would be like a shadow without a body.

The shouting grew louder, more desperate; and suddenly I heard a woman scream. Still I hesitated, but then I remembered what Cassia's father had said. There was a light in me that I had to learn to let out. He'd claimed that I could even work wonders then—

though I didn't think he had envisioned my challenging his entire clan.

Still, we'd all have to make the best of it. So Squeaky's one-man army charged down the street. I was in such a hurry that I almost passed by Cassia's lane. As it was, I came to a stumbling, undignified halt.

The Youngs all had their backs to me. I'd say there were about a hundred men, women, and even some excited children. I saw a number of wicked-looking spears; but there were even more hoes and sticks, and even a pot or two—as if they had picked up the first things that they could. I told myself that most of them wouldn't be any good in a fight; but as I stared at them, I couldn't shake this feeling in my stomach— like someone had grabbed my insides and was just twisting.

The few lanterns reddened the swaying heads of the mob, so they did not seem to belong to individual humans but instead seemed more like the ugly bumps on the back of some sick giant centipede that was trying to shove its way through Cassia's gates.

And above them all was Cassia. I could just make out her head and shoulders above her wall, as if she were standing on something. "The first one over the wall dies."

I recognized the voice of Stony coming not from

the front of the mob, but from its middle—as if he wanted people between himself and Cassia. "You can't shoot us all," he shouted. His voice sounded stretched out and thin—I think more with anger and fear than from the distance.

Cassia leaned the barrels of her gun on the wall and aimed. "But I can take quite a few. Who wants to be first?" When there wasn't any answer, Cassia raised the barrels contemptuously. "No, I didn't think so. You don't mind bullying one man and his family, but it's another thing to face demon bullets."

"Well, you can't bully a whole clan." Stony brandished a spear over his head and looked around. But at first it was only a few men behind him who yelled their agreement. The rest of the mob were looking at one another and murmuring as if they were trying to make up their minds. "How long are you going to let that girl get away with this?" he demanded, and looked around at the others for support.

He had to be stopped before he could whip up the mob any more. I wiped a sweaty palm on my shirt and twirled the spear so that the butt end was first. Filling my lungs with air, I started forward. "The Light," I shouted as I had at Canton. "The Light." And I thought once again of what the Gallant had said about the Darkness being more than the Manchus. I hadn't really understood what he'd meant before, but now I realized he had meant Stony's brand of stupidity as well. It was ignorance and prejudice and everything else that went along with it. And I was trying to keep the Light alive.

I pounded down the street. For once I was doing the right thing. With each step I felt stronger and quicker, as if I were drawing strength from the earth itself. Maybe it was the Gallant's doing. And the shouts felt like they were coming from within my soul now. And I knew I was doing the right thing. I was doing what I should have done the night Ducky died.

Cassia stared for a moment as if she couldn't quite believe her eyes and ears, and then she took up the joyful shout too. "The Light, the Light." She raised a hand and waved.

"The Light," I yelled back, and then I was in the middle of the mob. I had to strike hard and fast and think there were a dozen of us instead of one. I swung the spear back and forth, knocking arms and heads and shoulders. People tried to back away with frightened yelps and bumped into their neighbors, and the neighbors naturally tried to shove them away. In a few moments I had all the confusion that I could have wanted as the mob began to push and pull at one another.

I drove through them like I would have through a flock of ducks as I headed straight for the middle and Stony. All the time I could hear Cassia shouting, "The Light," and encouraging me for all she was worth.

I think in a normal fight Stony or any of his henchmen would have knocked me down easily, but they were confused. One moment they were facing just Cassia and her gun, and the next moment the crowd behind them was panicking. They couldn't know the reason. And then suddenly I was there attacking them. For all they knew, I could have been the first of a whole host of fighters. I clipped one man over the head so hard that he spun into the arms of another.

Then I jerked the spearhead up so that it was aimed right at Stony's throat. "I should kill you," I growled.

"Who are you?"

"The Light" was all that I said.

He gulped and swallowed. "What?"

"You wouldn't understand if I took a whole month to try to explain." Twirling my spear, I brought the shaft down against the side of his head, and Stony dropped unconscious, like a shadow puppet with broken guide sticks. Then I whirled the spear so that the people around us had to stumble backward. "Go home," I ordered.

"Yes, go home," Cassia repeated. And she set off one of the barrels of her gun. The explosion echoed in that small lane as if a thundercloud had come to squat there. I began to swing my spear again to add force to my order, and the mob disintegrated into individuals running out into the street.

Stony's henchmen were just taking it in that Cassia's rescuers consisted of only one man. I pointed the head of the spear at Stony. "Leave or he dies."

"You heard him." Cassia raised her gun again. "You all make a fine set of targets now."

They backed down the lane sullenly, like hungry dogs that had just gotten a beating when they'd been expecting a meal. When they were gone from the lane, I turned and bowed to the wall. "I'm sorry I'm late."

Cassia rested the butt of her gun on the wall. "I don't remember sending you an invitation to this party."

Now that the mob had cleared out, I could see a man sitting before the gates. A thin line of blood was trickling from his forehead into his eyes, while a kneeling boy was trying his best to stop it with a rag torn from his shirt. "I can't say much for your choice of party games."

Cassia peered down as if she were embarrassed about forgetting him. "Are you all right, Uncle Blacky?"

"Yes, it just looks worse than it is." He picked up a scholar's cap, and with the boy's help he stood up. "Next time I'll bring a spear instead of a speech— like this young man." He eyed me curiously.

"He . . . uh . . . fought with us in the war," Cassia said. Her head disappeared as she dropped down from the wall.

He shook off the boy's hands. "I'm fine now, Cricket," he said to the boy. I supposed that the boy was his son. He eyed me. "An odd sort of time to hold a reunion, isn't it?"

I glanced at the gates as I heard the bar being drawn back. "I just happened by."

"That's an amazing coincidence," the scholar observed.

Cassia came striding into the lane. "He's a Lau."

Uncle Blacky drew a deep breath and then let it out slowly. "You certainly pick a different sort of friend, Cassia."

"I take friendship where I can find it." She returned his stare boldly.

Tiny came out with a bandage around one hand and bruises over one side of his face. It must have been painful for him to smile, and yet he still tried. "There aren't many friends this brave."

Well, it was too late for Ducky, but I could take some small comfort in that. "I'm trying," I said, and then nodded toward Stony. "What should we do with him?"

Cassia took my arm. "Let's have a cup of tea first and then talk it over. If we're lucky, maybe he'll have crawled away and hidden under a rock." She smiled politely at Uncle Blacky. "Will you have some tea?"

Uncle Blacky was looking back and forth between us as if he were still having trouble taking it all in. "No, it's late. I think I'd rather get to my own bed. I prefer my excitement to come in a book."

Cassia patted his arm. "Thank you for trying to help. We'll talk tomorrow."

Uncle Blacky grinned slightly and started to limp down the lane. "Yes, it's so hard to have a serious chat at a big party like this."

Aster was inside the little courtyard. She cradled her baby, Otter, in one arm while the other held her coat shut. "Is it safe?" she asked Cassia.

"Yes, they're all gone for now—with Squeaky's help." Cassia actually smiled at me affectionately.

"Good." Aster's hand dropped from the jacket so that it fell open. Her blouse was bloody underneath the jacket. She brought her other hand up to support Otter as she lifted him toward Tiny. "Take him."

Tiny took the baby. "Why didn't you tell us?"

Aster gave a painful little grunt. "You were occupied."

"How did it happen?" Cassia dropped to her knees beside her friend.

Aster bit out her words as if each one cost her a great effort. "While we were trying to get back to the village . . . a knife."

"Lie down and I'll take care of it." Cassia began to lean forward to inspect the wound, but Aster stopped her.

"It's too late for that." When Aster began to sway, she grabbed hold of Cassia's arm. "Take care of them."

"I will," Cassia promised solemnly.

"Good." The breath left Aster in a deep sigh, and she just seemed to sag like a tired child falling asleep in Cassia's arms.

Chapter Fifteen

After we had carried Aster into the house, we left Tiny there to mourn while Cassia took Otter outside. As she jiggled the baby in her arms, she looked at me. "You should be getting back before it gets light."

My shoulders sagged as I remembered my own losses. "I can't. My clan saw me coming here."

"Oh, Squeaky." Cassia understood that I was more alone than she had ever been. She held Otter in the crook of one arm while she reached out her other to touch my shoulder.

I forced myself to smile. There'd been enough sadness tonight. "But it's all right. I've got the entire
Middle Kingdom to explore." I was determined to
make the best of things.

She used her hip to close the other gate. "With
whom?"

I closed the other as I studied her. What was she
suggesting? "I hadn't thought about company."

She nuzzled the soft, downy hair at the top of
Otter's head. "You should. It's a lonely road."

I lifted the bar. It was heavier than the usual ones,
but I guessed that Cassia had her reasons. At the
moment I felt more afraid than I had on the ridgetop
when I'd defied Lumpy. If I misunderstood Cassia,
would I insult her? Still, I had to risk it. "What's a
clown without an audience, right?"

She lifted a hand slowly, her eyes intent on my
face. "You're more than a clown. Clowns don't give
up everything to help others." She drew the backs of
her fingers almost wonderingly across my cheek. "You
gave up everything to help me."

I slid the bar through the holders. There was so
much to say to her that I didn't know where to begin.
It didn't seem possible that this was happening to me,
Squeaky. "It's going to be a long, hard road."

With a slow twist of her wrist, she brought her hand back to rest shyly on my chin. "Nothing has been easy in my life."

"And where will you live?" Tiny was standing in the doorway like some dark, determined storm cloud. "You can't stay here and you can't go to Phoenix Village."

I glanced at Cassia nervously. There really was so much still I wanted to say to her, but I didn't know where to start. But then I remembered what the Gallant had said about the land of the golden mountain so long ago. "Maybe I'll go to *America*. Your father said it's full of clanless people." The more I thought about it, the better I liked it. It'd be a chance to start all over.

Cassia's eyes widened in astonishment. "Are you crazy? If you survive the crossing, you may not survive the land. My brother's letters have been telling us all about the troubles over there. There have been so many of our people going overseas that the *Americans* have gotten scared. They're trying to drive us away. They passed a tax on foreign miners; but since most of the miners are T'ang people, it's really on us. A tax collector can do anything he likes to collect his money—kick, beat, even shoot a miner."

Tiny stepped out into the courtyard. "But Foxfire

also says that that will change. It's a land where their own laws say that everyone is equal."

Cassia looked over her shoulder wearily—as if this were an old argument between the two of them. "Even if that happened, there's our own people. When the *Americans* aren't fighting us, we're fighting among ourselves. There are so many T'ang people over there now that they've organized along the old lines, and that's revived the old feuds. The Fragrant Mountain men have been fighting pitched battles with the Three Districts people over there just like they would here."

"But Foxfire says that that will change too," Tiny insisted. "It's just a question of educating them in *American* principles."

I didn't know about political theory, but my uncle always said that money bought freedom.

Cassia slid her hand down to my shoulder. "There's always Hong Kong."

"And what will you do?" Tiny demanded. "How will you live? They say there's a half dozen people for every job." It was unsettling to hear the words pour from the quiet man like raindrops now—as if there were no way to ease his anger or his misery.

I knew from experience that Cassia could throw me easily to the ground, but now—as if I were made of fragile crystal—she timidly slipped an arm lightly around my waist. "I've got enough money for both of us."

I looked around the house. It was the same as any other farmer would have had. "Really?"

"I live simply," Cassia explained with all the dignity of an empress, "because I want to."

"The money isn't all yours," Tiny reminded her quietly. "Half of it belongs to your brother. You have to stay on to handle things until he comes back."

"Then I'll send for him," she tossed back defiantly.

Tiny flattened a palm against the air as if he wanted to shove her words back into her mouth. "You're not thinking straight. He probably couldn't drop everything and come back right away. He'll probably have to wind up things—and that's going to take a while. In the meantime, Squeaky and I could be earning money." Tiny clapped his hands and held them out. "In the land of the golden mountain. In just five years I could be rich. Then we could both live in Hong Kong in style."

"Or you could be dead." Cassia passed Otter to him. It seemed lost in Tiny's huge hands.

Almost instantly Otter began to cry, and Tiny began to jog him. "I could use a traveling companion—Squeaky?"

"I didn't think you were interested in becoming rich," I said to Tiny.

"It can't be any more dangerous over there than it is over here." Tiny jerked his head toward the street. "This is never going to happen again to me and mine. I'm going to be so rich that I can buy all the protection I want. I'm going to be so rich that that scum will have to lick my shoes." Tiny was patting his baby and making cooing noises. "You could be safe too."

Part of me wanted to accept Cassia's offer, but another part was drawn to the promise that Tiny was holding out to me. It would be nice to be rich on my own account—to see my village swallow whatever words they had said about Squeaky the Clown. I didn't want to be just Cassia's husband.

I put my arms around Cassia and gave her a quick, cautious hug. Uncle and I had rarely touched, so it was strange to show affection to anyone. "I don't like the idea of living off your money."

Cassia put her other arm around me and returned the hug, much to my surprise. "You'd expect me to live off your money if the situation were reversed."

"But it's not," I pointed out. I hastily held up a hand as Cassia sucked in her breath—as if I had just struck her in the stomach. "Before you say anything else, let's both agree on something."

Cassia drew back her shoulders. "What's that?" she asked cautiously.

I put my arm back around her to show her that I didn't mean any harm. "I don't think you're used to talking about these feelings any more than I am. We're like two people who have gone off their usual map."

Her body relaxed a little, but not much. "And we're just stumbling around in unknown territory."

I tightened my grip, but it was like holding a post now. We would be able to hold a discussion after all. "I know you like to plan people's lives; but for the first time in my life, I feel free."

She hunched like a crab trying to protect itself. "This isn't easy for me to say, because I've always prided myself on being independent. I've never needed anyone, but over the last few months I've come to depend on you."

"And I've enjoyed your company too," I admitted. "You've made me feel proud and good about myself."

She risked glancing at me sideways. "And you've made me feel . . ." She hesitated and then dipped her head to the side. ". . . well, human. Sometimes I've felt like an abacus—something that's just been good for calculating the value of land and crops. But I can talk to you."

My fingers felt the tight muscles of her back. "There's

a very sweet, caring person behind all those political speeches."

She raised her shoulders sharply. "But now you just want to go. It's like you can't wait to get away from me."

I pressed my nose against the side of her head. There was a faint smell of the demon gunpowder to her hair. "That's not it at all. Half of me would like to do things your way. But half of me can't. I've been a puppet all my life. I couldn't do anything unless someone else moved the sticks. I think I might find a home for us in *America*. At worst, I'll come with my own money. I'll be your equal."

She faced me finally, and I could see that there were tears hovering in the corners of her eyes. It startled me, because that was the last thing I thought a tough person like Cassia would do. "You mean I taught you too well?"

"It's your doing, you know. You're the one who wanted me to stand on my own feet and not care about what other people think." I grinned apologetically and was rewarded by a small smile.

"I should have stopped while I was ahead," she said. "But I just don't seem to know when to quit."

Tiny held the still-crying baby away from him as if he were at a loss to know what to do with the creature, and then I realized that he had probably been off at the uprising for most of Otter's life. "I could use a partner like you. I could sell my fields and we could use that for our passage money."

We stared at one another—each of us sensing the desperation in the other. We both needed to get away. "I've had my fill of stupidity."

"So have I."

Cassia clicked her tongue in exasperation and took Otter from Tiny. "I'll buy your fields. I'm the only one who'll give you a fair price." Almost instantly, the baby grew still.

Tiny scratched his head in puzzlement. "I was hoping you'd say that."

"You're showing more hope than sense." Resting Otter on her hip, she used her free hand to take my ear. "But if you're determined to go through with this, you're going to school."

It was a gentle but firm pressure that couldn't be denied, and I let myself be guided. "What school?"

"My brother's letters," she explained. "There's a lot you have to learn if you're going to survive the voyage over there and actually survive as a guest of the golden mountain."

"But you can't read," Tiny said.

"No, but I almost have them memorized," she said.

"And tomorrow I'll get Uncle Blacky and dictate some letters of introduction. There are people who can help you reach Foxfire."

Once Cassia had set her mind to help, she did it as thoroughly as only she could. After Aster's burial the next morning, she continued our lessons so that our heads were filled with information from her brother's letters. Then she turned us out of her house that afternoon when Uncle Blacky, the village scholar, came over. "Go on. Shoo. I've got letters to dictate."

I had a sudden twinge of conscience. "Can you also send a note to my uncle?"

"Yes, I could send it through a business associate." She paused with her hand on my back.

"Then tell him where I'm going," I instructed her.

"Nothing else?" she asked.

"Tell him, 'Once a fool, always a fool.' "

She gave me a small push toward the doorway. "You'll be surprised at how money can make a fool into a wise man."

As I walked with Tiny back to his house, I glanced over my shoulder. "She doesn't waste any time once she makes up her mind."

Tiny was making clucking noises to his baby. "She doesn't waste anything—money, land, or friends."

On the day we were supposed to leave, she brought

two bundles of food over to Tiny's. "Here. This should last you during your trip on the river."

Tiny set Otter's things down in the courtyard. He had his son in a basket under his other arm. "What about you? Will you be all right?" He handed his son to Cassia.

She took the basket. "Once you two are gone, they won't have any real targets. They'll give me looks, but I'm used to those."

I could only guess at what had happened when Cassia was a child; but if Three Willows was anything like my village, it couldn't have been too easy for someone as outspoken as she was. And her ideas couldn't have made her popular either. "I suppose," I said slowly, "that you're used to being alone."

She smiled down at Otter before she set his basket down on the ground. "I won't be alone." She spun her fingers in a slow circle. "Now turn around, both of you."

I eyed the two needles that she pulled from her hair. They were each as long as my index finger. "What for?"

"These may come in handy." She turned Tiny half around and slipped the needle into his queue at its base. "Just know where they are." She guided Tiny's hand up to the needle in his hair so that he could reach it anytime he wanted.

I pivoted obligingly. "Watch me sail back up the river in my golden ship."

She gave my queue a playful tug. "Wearing your coat of gold brocade and finger rings and nose rings and earrings and ankle rings of jade."

"Those too," I agreed.

She took my hand and held it up so I could feel the needle's tip. "What a fine spectacle that'll be."

I faced her again. "And because of my zealousness, Heaven will reward us with lots of children, and they'll all be scholars or rich."

She drew her fingertips over my face as if she were storing the contours away in her memory. "Heaven should grant us that. What would this world be without justice?"

"What would it, indeed?" I wondered.

Chapter Sixteen

Once we presented the first of our letters at the river port, the clerk was all smiles; and things went smoothly as we boarded the big river junk that slowly wound its way to the new city that the British demons were building. We would have liked to see as much of Hong Kong as we could, but we were herded right away into a barracoon.

In one of Foxfire's later letters, he had tried to describe the voyage for would-be travelers like myself and Tiny. The barracoons, at least, hadn't changed any since his day. I made a note to myself to tell

Cassia in the first letter I dictated. The one we entered was a long, dirty barracks where the beds were stacked in four tiers to the ceiling. The place was loud with shouting in all kinds of dialects, as if the barracoons were drawing men from all over the province.

They sat or lounged on the bare boards in a bored way or gambled listlessly. They didn't even bother to look at us as we squeezed past through the narrow aisles. Smoke just seemed to hang in the air, making it even harder to see in the dim light; and the place reeked of urine and feces and sweating bodies. Tiny wrinkled his nose. "I don't see any places. Let's try over there."

A young man in his twenties suddenly swung his leg from his bunk to block our way. He had almost no chin, and since he breathed through his mouth, his lips always seemed to be wriggling. "I think I smell a Stranger." He spoke in the dialect of the Fragrant Mountain district near Canton.

I spoke up before Tiny could. "It didn't matter at Canton. We were glad of anyone's help." I looked all around, hoping that someone might have picked up my cue.

A man across from him suddenly looked up from his dominoes game. He was sucking at a water pipe, though it had no tobacco. "I was there. We had one common enemy." His finger sketched the word for "three" on the side of his bunk. It was a sign of the Brotherhood.

Remembering what Cassia had done at the tavern, I held three fingers parallel to the floor. "The light could be better in here."

A second man lounged against the beds. He was using a splinter to pick his teeth. "Yes, it's too dark."

I leaned my elbow against a tier, trying to appear more relaxed than I felt. "I don't know about the light, but I hear it's healthier overseas." I'd have to be sure to tell Cassia about how I'd remembered.

"It's easy to lose one's head here in the dark," the first man, Dominoes, agreed. He spoke in the dialect of the Three Districts while the second man, Splinters, spoke in the dialect of the Four Districts. The Brotherhood was the only group that seemed to cut across district lines.

The man who had blocked our way looked down at his leg as if he wished he could have cut it off right then. "It was just a joke."

Splinters jabbed his makeshift toothpick at the chinless man. "Listen, Mister— What's your name, anyway?"

"Carp." The chinless man gulped. It was a good nickname for him.

"Well, Carp, I think you'd better find another way to make people laugh." Splinters kicked Carp's leg out of our way. "Fragrant Mountain men stink like Manchus."

"I'm against the Manchus too," Carp insisted shrilly. "I detest them. I spit on them."

Dominoes cut him short with a gesture. "Your folk agreed to collect the tax among the guests of the golden mountain when the Manchus wanted money to help end the 'party' at Canton. I can't see any reason to pay the troops that are massacring my kin."

Carp shook his head violently. "My people don't have any more reason to love the Manchus than you do. The village leaders thought they could gain some influence with the Manchus."

"Your folk would do anything for money." Splinters grabbed him by the front of his shirt.

I stopped him. "He's not worth the trouble."

Splinters stared at me for a moment, and then he let Carp collapse back on his bed. "No, I guess he isn't." He wiped his hand with deliberate thoroughness on the front of his shirt. "Come on." He jerked a dirty thumb to our left. "I'll take you to a place where you'll find better company—over that way."

We followed him through the barracoons to a section near a window where there were actually some empty bunks. "We keep these for brothers."

"So where did you join?" Splinters asked us in a low voice.

Cassia had given us some information about the Brotherhood; but in the short time we'd had, she couldn't tell us everything, and I doubt we could have remembered it all even if she had. Tiny glanced at me. We were in even worse trouble now. The Brotherhood wouldn't take kindly to our imitating the brothers.

But then I remembered some of the things that Cassia had said about her father, and I decided to take a chance. "It's lighter here." I pitched my bundle on the boards of an empty bed. "It'll be nice when the Light fills the world. At least, that's what the Gallant always used to say."

Splinters studied us cautiously. "I knew a fellow by that name. He was quite a runner."

"He might have been at one time," Tiny said quickly, "but when I knew him he had a limp."

Splinters seemed satisfied, and I realized that we

were being tested. "There was none better." I could see we had both gone up in his estimation.

And I thought I'd remember this moment for the first letter that I'd send to Cassia. Long after his death, the Gallant was still protecting us.

"He didn't have the luck," Dominoes said. He must have finished his game. "If you don't have the luck, it's no use trying."

"You want to know what real luck is?" Splinters snorted. "I heard about a pair of Three Districts men. They were just clerks in a store overseas when they heard about the gold strike, so they went up into the hills. They'd never touched a hand to dirt, and yet the earth liked them. They went up and bought a claim that the demons said was worthless because they'd never gotten more than a nail-size bit of gold from the claim. And then they found the nugget."

"How much did it weigh?" I asked. "A kilo?"

Splinters jerked his head at me. "Forty."

Tiny shook his head. "Don't try to play jokes on us. How could the demons overlook anything that big?"

Splinters dismissed Tiny with a wave of his hand. "That shows you how much you know. There's an awful lot of ground to dig in a claim. The demons were just millimeters away when they gave up."

Dominoes clapped his hand on Splinters's shoulder and smiled patronizingly. "Excuse me, brother. It was two men from the *Four* Districts who found the nugget, and it weighed *fifty* kilos."

"Pardon me," another brother said, "but it was a pair from the Three Districts—only the nugget weighed a hundred kilos."

A fourth brother spoke up then. "No, it was two hundred kilos."

"I never heard that one." Splinters frowned.

"It's the truth," the fourth man swore. "These boys were smart. They didn't want the news getting around before they could get away, so they got some chisels and cut the nugget into small pieces." He looked around and added as the topper, "A brother of a friend of mine helped them."

The others clapped their hands in wonder at a gold nugget that size. I leaned my head against one of the tiers and watched the others. Splinters preferred to believe in a story about a two-hundred-kilo nugget rather than in his own story of a forty-kilo one. So did all the others.

The brothers shipped out about three days before

we did—which was just as well, since I didn't know how long I could keep up the masquerade. There was bound to be trouble wherever they went, but I'd worry first about getting overseas.

While we waited, we tried to stay out of gambling games. Foxfire had warned that sometimes would-be guests were coaxed to gamble and add onto their debts. Most of them were getting their passage through the credit-ticket system, in which they promised to repay their fares with interest. But sometimes extras would be added on—like the cost of outfitting a hold with water tanks and bunks. Through the sale of Tiny's fields, we were going over as paid passengers, so we would have a choice of jobs once we reached *America*.

And all the time we were in the barracoons I would hear over and over again about the lucky pair who found the huge nugget—though it had grown to the size of three hundred kilos by the time I'd left.

The story was like a weed that had sunk its roots deep into the soil, and pull and dig and chop at it as much as you liked, you could only pull out the stems. The roots would always be sending a fresh new plant out again. Well, maybe a couple of men really had found a forty-kilo nugget once—and maybe even one of three hundred kilos. But not one man in the bar-racoons stopped to ask how many other T'ang men would ever find another such nugget.

Was I just on some fool's chase after all? Should I have done what Cassia had said and gone with her to Hong Kong? No, I told myself, you've got to believe in yourself. That's the first thing she would've said to me.

Chapter Seventeen

It seemed to take forever for us to be assigned to a ship, but finally it was our turn along with some four hundred others.

Our interpreter was a small rat of a man, the child of a T'ang woman and a *Portuguese* demon; and he spoke with a thick accent that made it hard to understand him at first. But he made it clear that we would be interviewed by a Manchu official who would ask us if we were going voluntarily—to which we were supposed to answer yes. It was just as Foxfire had described it, so I began to have this strange feeling of following in his footsteps.

When that was done, we were allowed to board the ship. It was a large ship—far larger than the junk that had carried us down here—and it had sleek, curved lines that reminded me of a beetle that had been tipped over; but it was still hard to believe that they were going to fit all four hundred of us into the ship.

It took a while to board the ship, because the demon sailors searched everyone's belongings and confiscated anything that might be considered a weapon. I was a little nervous about Cassia's gift, but the sailors never looked in my queue. They were in too much of a hurry, because there were so many of us to get into the boat. They also missed a good many knives and daggers—as it turned out during the voyage.

After trying to pack my things back into my bundle, I began to climb down the stairs. What little light was in the hold came from the lamp hanging from the ceiling. The hold itself was filled with tiers of bunks packed even closer than they had been in the barracoons, and the air seemed still and dark. I turned to Tiny. "It smells worse than the barracoons."

"Don't stall," the interpreter shouted impatiently.

"Move all the way into the back." And a demon sailor shook a club at us menacingly.

But Foxfire had mentioned, and Cassia had stressed, that above everything else we should try to get bunks near the hatchway. I didn't really want to create a scene, but I had the feeling of being guided by Foxfire's invisible hand. Instead of heading into the back, I dumped my bundle on a top bunk to the left of the stairs; and Tiny immediately flung his things on a bunk to the right.

"No, move on," the interpreter yelled down to us.

But I climbed up and lay down, hoping that Foxfire's advice was worth all the trouble. For a moment I thought the interpreter was going to send some sailors down after us; but the demon captain was impatient to finish boarding the rest of us, and he barked something to the interpreter; and the line of men continued to squeeze through the narrow aisles between tiers.

It took most of the day to board us; and as soon as that was done, iron grates were pulled over the hatchway and sailors stood guard with guns. The interpreter said they were afraid that we were pirates, but men only laughed at him. "They're just afraid of what will happen when we get the putrid water and the spoiled food," one man hooted back.

The air itself was hot and muggy most of the time; and as soon as we set sail, it got worse. Everyone, except for the placid Tiny, who seemed above such things, got sick; and the sides of the tiers were thick with vomit. It mixed on the floor with the contents of the slop buckets that overturned.

The sailors weren't completely without feeling. They rigged up a small sail that sent a breeze into the hold, but unfortunately it never carried beyond a few tiers. I was glad then that Cassia had beaten it into our heads to get the bunks we had. I'd have to thank her in the first letter I dictated to her.

Men tried to sleep on the stairs, but they were so crammed together that a fight broke out among them. The demon sailors broke it up, swinging the butts of their rifles crazily. Then they picked the first man they could and dragged him up on deck. All of us within the hold listened in silence to the hiss of the whip and the man's screams. When they were finished, the demon sailors left him at the top of the stairs and the interpreter called down to us to take him back to his bunk. Men from his district helped him to his place—only to find that someone had stolen everything he had owned.

That was when Tiny rolled over and looked at me

across the aisle. "I think we're going to need Cassia's gifts tonight."

I thought there might be trouble too, since we were in the most desirable bunks. I looked around at the others near us. We ate in groups in one of several cooking places. "Maybe we should take turns on watch," I said to everyone in general.

But they all pretended to ignore me. If they were like the typical villager, they probably suspected me because they didn't know me and would automatically assume that I was trying to cheat them somehow.

Finally, Tiny sighed. It was just him and me again. "I'd like the second watch."

"Fine," I said. "I'll thump on the boards of my bed if there's trouble."

That night I lay on my bunk tensely. Occasionally I heard the sound of threshing and a muffled cry. Shadows twisted wildly on the walls of the hold, moving back and forth rhythmically to the swinging of the lamp.

Suddenly a man rose on my right. As I reached for the needle in my queue, I kicked out with my foot. Usually I made a pillow from my cloth shoes, but tonight I'd kept them on for just such a need.

But my foot missed and the man grabbed my ankle, and I was dragged halfway out of my bunk.

Desperately I grabbed at his queue, which dangled over his shoulder. It was hard to grasp because it was so greasy. I don't think the man had ever washed it in his life. But still I managed to yank on it, and the man's head thumped hard against the boards. He fell down on the floor.

Across from me I heard a yell, and a man was tumbling back, clutching his shoulder. Tiny was leaning over, the needle in his hand. "What do you think of Cassia's lessons now?" He grinned at me. "She taught us well about what Foxfire said."

"I'm becoming impressed with Foxfire." I listened to the men shuffle down the aisle into the shadows. I'd never been in a situation where I had a feeling that everyone was my enemy. Thank Heaven for Tiny's company. Without him, I would have felt like one more dog snarling at all the others. "But not everyone has the benefit of her instructions. I wonder how many bunks are going to change hands tonight?"

Tiny tapped his needle against the side of his bunk. The needle was yet another thing to mention to Cassia when I finally dictated that letter to her. "Not these two, at least." He rolled over onto his back. "My boy had better appreciate this."

As it turned out, there were two bunks that changed hands. The bodies of the two former owners were left by the stairs, and the demon sailors took them away and tossed them over the side when they brought us our day's ration of water and food.

Then one morning the grate was jerked back and the interpreter strutted importantly down the steps. "All right, you filthy rats, it's time to bathe." He began to point. "You, you, you." Behind him a sailor with a club gestured toward the deck. He seemed to be just waiting for an excuse to use the club on someone who was slow to disobey. "No, don't bother taking your things," the interpreter said. "There'll be a sailor standing guard."

I stumbled up with the others on the deck, grateful to look up at the sky. Hugh white clouds hovered like balls of cotton, and between them I could see patches of bright-blue sky. "So Heaven's still there," I said to Tiny.

"So are the guns," he said. Sailors had taken up positions around us. They were armed with clubs and guns.

"Hey, where do we put our clothes?" someone shouted to the interpreter. He started to take off his shirt. "Hey, I'm talking to you." But the interpreter paid no more attention to him than he would have to

some barking dog. The interpreter just marched behind the line of sailors.

I shivered as a wind blew across the deck. "I'm
more interested in the water. Where are the buckets?"

Suddenly a team of sailors took up the hose while
another group gathered around a pump and began to
work it. Tiny stared at them. "They're not going to
do what I think they are."

Water suddenly spurted from the hose. The column played down the line too fast for us to dodge.
It felt like someone had struck me in the chest, and
when I gasped, I took in a mouthful of saltwater. I
began to choke. I could hear Uncle saying that it was
just like me to drown on board a ship.

And suddenly the water stopped. Wheezing, I got
my breath back and looked up to see that Tiny had
stepped in front of me and was blocking the water.
He stood there with his legs spread, his body sometimes shaking with the force; but try as the sailors
could, they could not force him back.

The captain gave some kind of angry yip, and the
sailors eventually switched the hose to someone else.
Tiny turned his back to them and so did I. He grinned
at me as the water dripped down from his nose and
chin. "Next time keep your mouth closed."

The sailors howled and cackled with laughter as

they played the water over us. Those who tried to run or hide only made themselves into targets, because the sailors around the hatchway would shove them back so that the sailors with the hose could give them special attention. "My shirt, my shirt," shouted the man who had tried to question the interpreter.

I didn't see it around, so I suppose it had been sprayed over the side. The next thing I knew, the interpreter was shouting for us to go back down; and we made our way like drowned rats back down into the hold. The sailor with the gun had stayed on the steps so that no one had tried to steal our things or take our bunks.

When I woke the next morning, there was a dead man on the steps. Even as I watched, two sailors guarded by a third sailor with a gun came down the steps and lifted the body. A moment later I heard a splash as the body was tossed over the side.

I swung my legs from my bunk and looked at Tiny. "I wonder how many more are going to end their trip that way?"

"More than I like to think," he said.

I made my way over to one of the buckets of night soil. It had overflowed as usual. I did my business anyway and started to make my way back when I heard a groan. It was Carp, the young man who'd tried to block our way in the barracoons. He was lying bare chested, too weak to move his head away from a puddle of his own vomit. His feet were bare, and I didn't see any belongings. I looked around, wondering which of his neighbors had stolen his things while he lay sick and helpless.

"This man needs help," I said. But the others pretended that they hadn't heard me. Some of them stared up at the bunks above them. Others went on chatting quietly to one another. As before, it was every man for himself.

I looked around. We were perhaps fifteen meters from the hatchway, but we might as well have been a kilometer. Among the hulking bunks, the light was only a thin crack; and the air was hot and still, with thick, stinking smells.

Of course, that wasn't my business. I had no reason to help him. I had myself to watch out for. I started on, but I couldn't help wondering what would have happened to me if the Gallant had thought that way. As he had said to Cassia, we had to live the Light. I was sure that his daughter would have approved. It was funny, but once you got started doing the right thing, it got easier to do.

When I got back to my bunk, I began to gather up my things. "What are you doing?" Tiny demanded.

"I'm going to switch bunks for a while."

Tiny leaned forward so he could sit up. "Who is it?"

"Remember that fellow who tried to give us a hard time in the barracoons?" I closed the lid on the basket. "Well, he's sick."

Tiny stared at me in disbelief. "Him? If you ask me, you're the sick one."

"I'm tired of seeing us at one another's throats over every little advantage. I'm tired of treating everyone like an enemy. It's time we realized that we have more in common than not." I raised one hand. "We're all fingers on the same hand. It's only by uniting that we can be strong." I closed my fingers into a fist.

Tiny turned away so that he was lying on his side. "There's more than one sick man."

"We have to make a start somewhere. The Gallant said that we have to live the Light." I picked up my basket.

"I could use a change of scenery too," a man said from my right. It was the fellow who'd lost his shirt when we'd been "bathing." He slid from his bunk and began to gather up his things. "The faces around here are too ugly."

"They call me Squeaky," I said.

"Bright Star." He nodded to me.

Another man sat up. "I don't want to sleep next to a sick man."

"Then move," Tiny grunted. The bunk bed creaked as he started to pick up his things as well.

"You're coming too?" I looked up at him.

"The Gallant was my friend," Tiny said simply.

By the end of the day, we had a half dozen others who also switched. It wasn't easy moving backward into that ovenlike hold amid the heat and the smells. People looked at us as if we were crazy when we switched bunks temporarily, and most refused to help us care for the sick. But a few, a very few, chose to live the Light.

We even got some of the others to help out on occasion when it came to trying to keep the hold clean and moving the buckets to the hatchway on a regular basis. That much, at least, was in their own self-interest.

More men died during the voyage—some of disease, some in the fights that burst out during the long, cramped, boring voyage; others died during the night— their throats cut and their belongings stolen. But I like to think that a few more men made it overseas thanks to what we did.

Chapter Eighteen

San Francisco was very different from the city that Foxfire had described in his first letters some five years ago. For one thing, there were far more permanent buildings, including a bank made of stone shipped from the Middle Kingdom and built by our people for the *Americans*.

Over here the groups of T'ang people had organized themselves by areas, so once we got through the warehouse that the demons used for Immigration, we could hear one man shouting, "Four Districts over here" while another was shouting for men from the Three

Districts around Canton. A third was shouting for Strangers.

Tiny hesitated.

"Go where you need to," I said.

He took my bundle and hefted it onto his shoulder as well. "What would Otter say if I let something happen to his Uncle Squeaky?"

We rode in wagons up to the headquarters of the Four Districts, past buildings of two and even three stories that were all jammed together on the hills like giant hogs huddling against the wind. But we were the lucky ones who found places on the wagon. Others had to trek in single file up the hill into the town.

The T'ang people's town was a strange place. They had taken the tall, boxlike American buildings and made them into their own. Big wooden signs in red or black with gold words had been hung on their fronts beneath ornate metal balconies, and from the balconies hung paper lanterns or even bronze ones. I'd hoped that I could still carry out my own plan and settle with Cassia in the land of the golden mountain, but everything seemed so jammed together that I knew Cassia could never be happy in the city. I'd have to find someplace else.

The headquarters for the Four Districts men was

a big place with a small temple and a dormitory that, though crowded, was clean at least. Once there, I presented another of Cassia's letters of introduction to a clerk, and again felt the long reach of Foxfire's shadow. Much to my surprise, we found ourselves whisked into the room of one of the chief officers.

The office was filled with heavy teak furniture and drawers and cabinets crammed with papers and books. There were two chairs in front of the desk, but they were filled with papers and books as well. Art objects were tucked away in odd corners or sat on top of piles of old newspapers. There was even a box of snuff bottles exquisitely carved from rare crystals. Beside the box was a small set of empty shelves, as if shelves and bottles were waiting for a time to be put up on the wall. In the middle of the cluttered desk was an odd demonic clicking contraption. Its front was occupied by a white circle divided into twelve parts. Two metal rods projected from the center—the short one didn't move at all while I studied it, but the longer one moved a fraction.

I turned around to Tiny. "What do you suppose this is?"

But before Tiny could reply, the door opened and a young man about his age bustled into the room. He was dressed in western trousers that must have been tailored to fit him tightly, the way that demons seemed to favor. Over a demon shirt of white, though, he wore a black T'ang vest of silk and a small merchant's cap.

"It's a demon clock," the young man explained. He must have overheard me through the door. "Time is almost as precious to them as gold, so one of our hours would make two of theirs; and then they divide that hour up into sixty parts, and each of those parts into sixty more."

I moved away from the contraption, feeling as if it could steal part of my own life. "Fancy that."

The young man brusquely shoved a pile of papers from a chair and motioned for Tiny to sit down. "Please excuse the clutter. I just never seem to have the time to set up my office the way I want. My name's Smiley."

I examined the snuff bottles and found that they were the animals of the zodiac. "It's a shame to leave these in a box."

"Those old things?" Smiley cleared a stack of books from a chair for me. "I keep seeing better ones each month. I'm waiting until I finally decide on what ones I want to display."

I held up one bottle of some translucent stone where the red hung like mist. It was a carving of a serpent.

"Excuse me, but it's hard to believe that there are bottles better than this."

"We guests are used to more sorts of excitements than even men from Canton are used to." Smiley looked around as if unsure where to put the books. They seemed to be in some demonic script.

I put the bottle back. "You're learning *American*?"

"They're just primers." Smiley finally gave up and just dumped them on the floor.

"I have to admire such ambition." I sat down on the chair.

"There's no limits here like back in the Middle Kingdom." Smiley plopped down in his chair. "But it's good to be able to sit for a bit."

I shook my head. "All these wonderful things and you can't enjoy them."

"Now I can really believe that you're a friend of Foxfire's." He studied me the way a scholar might scrutinize a rare text. "He's an important man over here. They say he has the luck. There can't be any other explanation for how he does it."

I was still trying to find a comfortable position in the heavy, ornately carved teak chair that I'd been given. "Does what?"

"You mean you don't know?" Smiley regarded us suspiciously.

"He's careful what he says in his letters." Tiny frowned.

Smiley thought for a moment. "Yes, silly of me to think he'd put something like that in a letter that would pass through many hands before its gets home."

"But what does he do?" I repeated.

Smiley flung out his arms. "Why, nothing but absolute magic. He takes a field that everyone says is played out, and he brings bag after bag of gold out of it. It's as if he's found the secret of turning dirt into precious metal."

Tiny scratched his head. "Fancy that. That is a good trick."

Smiley sat back slowly in his chair. "You're a Stranger?"

"I come from the Four Districts," Tiny corrected him politely but firmly.

Smiley pressed his fingertips together. "You mean Foxfire never wrote about the troubles over here?"

Tiny smiled with one corner of his mouth. "Which troubles?"

Smiley rested his chin on top of his fingers. "Yes, true. But I'm referring to here. This is no longer the rich province it was originally. We have to protect our members' interests." He folded his hands together. "Our people wouldn't take it kindly if we helped a Stranger. You're men of the world. You understand."

Tiny and I exchanged glances. It was the same old garbage that had been dumped over here. "You're refusing to help Tiny?"

Smiley flipped his fingers in the air. "Oh, we'll send someone to escort him to the headquarters of the Strangers."

I tapped my fingers against his fancy desktop. "There can't be competition for the played-out fields, and those are the ones we'll be interested in." I settled back with a triumphant smile. "Besides, I don't think Foxfire would take it kindly if you turned out his friend Tiny."

"Foxfire and I go back a long way." Tiny stuck out one foot in front of the other. "Long enough for me to remember a set of letters written for him by his sworn brother, Smiley. But you quarreled."

"I was . . . um . . . organizing what I was doing," Smiley said distantly—as if that belonged to another life. "He couldn't see that we needed discipline."

"What sort of discipline?" I wondered. He was reminding me of the excuses Stony had used for attacking the Strangers.

"Whatever is necessary to teach them a lesson," Smiley said carefully.

His words made me shiver. He might have had more elegant trappings, but he reminded me a lot of Lumpy. I was beginning to think that we might have escaped one set of dangers to wander into another—like jumping over a fire only to land in a pit of snakes.

Still, this area of discussion wasn't going to get us any closer to Foxfire. I tried to think of how Cassia would handle a situation like this, and then I had it. Though it made me uncomfortable to depend on Foxfire again, I used his name for an appeal. "Help us—for old time's sake," I urged.

Smiley sat there as if he were trying to think of some response, but finally he just jerked out a strange-looking pen that must have been demonic. It had a single steel triangle at its tip rather than a brush. The triangle looked like a fang. "Very well. Both Tiny and I are taking big risks." He dipped the pen into a bottle of blue ink and scratched something in quick strokes on a heavy sheet of paper. "We'll do what we can to see that you reach Foxfire intact. After that, it's up to him." He restored the pen to a holder. "But in order to get you there, I have one request: Tiny must keep his mouth shut so people won't know that he's a Stranger."

I glanced at Tiny. He shrugged massively. "All

right," I said, "but we'll also need to dictate a letter."

"I'll do it myself." Smiley eagerly took out a fresh sheet of paper.

Suddenly I realized that anything I said would be known to everyone here, so I though better about it. "No, it can wait till we reach Foxfire."

He seemed almost disappointed. "Suit yourself."

I will say this much for Smiley: He hurried our passage inland as if he were eager to get rid of us, but he was also conscientious about it. He saw that we were outfitted in pants of some heavy, blue demon cloth called *denim* and heavy casings of leather that were the demon fashion for boots. He even saw to it that we had black felt hats—like the other old-time guests.

At the appointed time he took us down to the docks himself to the riverboat that would take us upriver. I had been expecting something like the junk that had taken us to Hong Kong, but instead I saw a boat that was more like a floating house with a big paddle wheel in the stern.

Leading us around to the stern, he saw us safely aboard with the other T'ang men going into the gold country. "Give my regards to Foxfire," Smiley said, "and good luck to both of you. You're going to need it."

"Thank you." I started to nod my head to him, but he stopped me.

"You're in *America* now. Say good-bye their way." He thrust out his hand. "Take it." When I obeyed reluctantly, he pumped his arm up and down. "There. Now it's official." He took Tiny's hand and shook it just as hard. "Be careful."

As I watched Smiley hurry toward the gangplank, I murmured to Tiny, "I bet he's breathing a sigh of relief."

Chapter Nineteen

"So it's you," said a voice from behind me. It was Carp. "I might have known I couldn't get away from you two until you got a thank-you."

"Believe me," I said as I sat down beside him, "we've got other things on our mind."

But Carp was like one of those small dogs that bark all the louder the more embarrassed they are. "Believe me, I'd rather stay in the city, but everyone said I had to join my father in Eden." It was as if he blamed us for all his troubles because we were the nearest target.

"Eden?" I raised an eyebrow and sighed heavily. "It looks like we're going to be neighbors then. It seems as if only the finest people are going to that little resort."

Carp nudged Tiny. "You could at least ask how I'm doing."

"Tiny's got laryngitis," I said quickly.

Carp was a sharp boy who could figure out things for himself. For a moment I thought he was going to give us away, but I guess he figured he'd pay us back for the voyage. "Well." He grinned. "I suppose Squeaky can talk enough for two."

Though it was hot in the city, it was cool on the bay; and though its waters were calmer than the ocean, our boat was smaller, so that we felt each choppy wave as it tossed the boat's bow up. It didn't take long before all of us were sick all over again.

Things didn't get any better until we passed into the second of two smaller bays. Marshland marked the mouth of the river that the boat entered. We then churned up a wide river past lush meadows burned a golden color by the sun. In the bright daylight the fields almost seemed to shimmer with a secret fire.

I tried to feel what Foxfire had described. To him, the golden meadows had been like fur stretched taut over the muscles of our new home. And that had only added to his enthusiastic optimism—as if he could tame and ride the land; and the more energetic the land, the longer and better the ride.

"Look at how black that soil is," I said to Tiny. "I bet you could grow anything there."

Tiny nodded his head in agreement, but Carp merely looked at me in a superior way. "You can take the boy away from the farm, but you can't take the farm away from the boy."

But I couldn't help comparing the little scraps of land that Uncle Itchy toiled over to the virgin soil all around me. Our valleys must have been as rich as this at one time, though now they were old and tired. I could almost feel the life trying to burst through the soil. If it wasn't so isolated, I thought, Cassia would love to have a farm here. But perhaps there was someplace with T'ang people where we could farm. It was a promising sign at least. I'd give Cassia my own account of the country the first chance I got. "This is where the real gold is," I said. "This is what I would like to own."

"The demons would never let you," Carp said matter-of-factly.

"I can still dream," I snapped.

Eventually the river forked, and we went up a broad, lazy river where the bushy, green banks slid slowly by. In Marysville we got off to join the hundreds of others trekking into the gold country. But a letter from Smiley helped us get a lift on a supply wagon going up to Eden; and even though Carp was poor company, we took him along.

The wagon bumped along a rutted dirt road past fields where the ground seemed to rise and fall like ocean swells. Here and there in some hollow, a lone tree grew like a bright-green island.

Our driver was dressed like a typical guest in heavy woolen demon shirt and pants of *denim*. He had a hat like we did, but his feet were encased in tight black boots that went all the way up to his knees, so everyone called him Boots.

He'd been here since the very beginning of the gold rush, and he'd just said good-bye to a friend who had come over when he had. "Now as for me," Boots told us good-humoredly, "I won't go home until I can buy an orchard of trees with peaches that will make you immortal. And I'll have a garden with hidden grottoes and waterfalls and all the kinds of beautiful things that a person can buy."

I decided that it would be better to be formally polite. "Excuse me. I'm only an ignorant—"

"No, no, don't stand on ceremony." Like many guests, Boots disliked the excessive politeness of home.

I gripped a rope that held a heavy crate to the wagon bed. "All right then. Why stay here?"

Boots looked over his shoulder at me. "Why go back and get stuck on some farm with just pigs for company when I can stay here and see the best acrobats and puppeteers and concerts and operas right here?"

I thought of Smiley. "And surround yourself with beautiful things."

Boots flicked the ends of the reins against his horse's rump. "All the ships of the world come to San Francisco, and they bring the best of everything—including the news of the world. Ask me about the *British*. Ask me about the T'ai-p'ings. I may not know about the gossip back in my old village, but I know everything that's worth knowing about the whole Middle Kingdom."

"But this still isn't your home," I pointed out.

"Sometimes," Boots informed me loftily, "there are more important things than home. Only the best of things come to you here."

I was silent while I mulled that one over. I felt almost as if I'd been brought up to a mountaintop where the whole world had been spread out beneath me. But was it what I wanted?

I watched the soil begin to give way to blunt rocks

that reared upward like dark-nosed sharks. And as the ground rose into hills, the rocks began to increase until I felt as if I were surrounded.

But as the hills increased in size, we began to see more trees with funny, twisting trunks and small rubbery green leaves like frozen drops. And in the distance, we could see a ridge with steep, sharp sides as if it were a slice of some dark cake. Tall pine trees lined its top.

"That's Eden up there. We're going to have to pass through the American side first," he warned us. "No matter what they do, don't talk back or do anything that would give them an excuse to attack."

I glanced at Tiny. Things were beginning to sound as dangerous as when we'd been on the run from the Manchus. Tiny simply sighed, and then raised and lowered his hands helplessly. This was the other side of our new home. As beautiful and splendid as it could be, it was also wild and dangerous. It could be like riding a tiger. At the very least, it didn't sound like any place to live with Cassia.

I could feel all my hopes and plans for a life with Cassia here beginning to collapse. "But don't they have laws here?"

"They do." Boots held the reins lightly in one hand while he reached a hand into one of his big demon boots. "But they don't apply to us. An *American* robber came into a T'ang camp and shot one of the miners. The others captured him and they took him to the sheriff, but the sheriff had to let the robber go. He said there were no legal witnesses."

"What about the T'ang miners?" I demanded. More and more, it didn't sound like a place for Cassia—or for me.

Boots took out a dirty rectangle of what smelled like tobacco. "They were the wrong skin color. Non-whites can't testify in the courts. They need an *American* witness."

Carp made a small sign against evil. "What did my father get me into?"

Boots didn't answer until he had worried off a bite from the rectangle of tobacco. "It's their country." His words came out muffled around that big bite of tobacco. "But then they turn around and blame us because we don't sink any roots into this country."

"Then maybe we should get out," Carp said.

"For what?" The bite of tobacco made a funny lump behind Boot's cheek as he talked. "Just so you can go home and be bossed around by everyone— from the Manchus on down to the clan elders and your own family?"

Tiny, though, clapped his hand on my knee as if to reassure me. Cassia had tried to warn us.

"Well," I said, "I guess we've survived worse." But I hunkered down deeper among the sacks and boxes for whatever protection they could give. In his letters Foxfire had warned about such troubles, but he hadn't described how helpless a person could feel. This was their land, after all, and we were here as their guests. It sounded like they could do most anything they wanted—but that didn't sound like the "best of everything" that Boots had bragged about.

It took most of the day to reach Eden. There wasn't much more to the *American* side than two dozen buildings of weathered, unpainted lumber. The roofs were covered with those flat shingles that the *Americans* favored. They reminded me somehow of an animal flattening its fur in sullen anger. *Americans* stared at us from the windows and the doors. They were dressed in rough, dirty clothes, and their faces were covered with whiskers or even beards.

It took me a moment to realize that they were staring—no, glaring at us. Boots was sitting rigid on the buckboard, refusing to look either to the right or to the left. "Easy now," he whispered to us. "Remember what I said."

But a frightened Carp started to rise from the rice sacks. "Why are you going so slow?"

Boots, however, didn't say anything. He just kept chewing at his tobacco as if his life depended on it.

"Because we can't let them know that we're afraid," I said in a low voice. And reaching a hand up, Tiny grabbed his shoulder and forced him down.

Most of the *Americans* went back to whatever they were doing, but there were two of them who began to yelp and make snarling noises—like dogs quarreling over a bone.

"Good Heavens, they've got guns." Carp's eyes were wide.

"They're not using them." I helped Tiny hold him down. No, I couldn't invite Cassia here. She would already have been shooting it out with them.

"One of them's getting a rock." Carp struggled to get free from Tiny's grip but couldn't.

"Look at how he's staggering," I grunted. "He's drunk. He can't hit anything."

"Watch out." Carp ducked anyway as a rock whizzed by some three meters away. There was the crash of breaking glass.

"Correction," I murmured from one corner of my mouth. "He can still hit the side of a house."

We left the *Americans* quarreling among themselves as the wagon rounded a bend. "We made it." Carp sighed in relief.

"You're not home yet" was all that Boots would say.

It was about a kilometer to the town of the T'ang people. The buildings were the same as the ones in the *American* side of town; but these were built all in a row as if huddling together for protection. In front of the buildings were about a hundred T'ang men divided into two groups and they were busy shouting at one another and throwing stones.

Boots stopped about two hundred meters from the town. "This is as far as I go until that commotion is over."

I rose in the back of the wagon and craned my head to try to see better. "What's this fight about?"

Boots set the brake with both hands. "Most likely they're arguing over that new tax."

"To end the . . . uh . . . 'party' at Canton?"

Boots wrapped the reins around the brake. "You don't have to use euphemisms anymore, boy. Most everyone over here is against the Manchus."

"Including me," Carp was quick to say.

Boots reached into his boot again. "I suppose it was expensive for the Manchus to put down the Canton uprising, but suppressing the T'ai-p'ing rebellion is costing even more."

The T'ai-p'ings had been started by a Stranger who had mixed together a lot of demon religion and T'ang politics. Though he had begun their rebellion in the province to the west of ours, they had spread northward quickly. Though I didn't know much more about them than that, I hoped they'd give the Manchus as much trouble as they could handle.

I shook my head when he held his tobacco out to me. "We're not paying, I hope." After what I'd seen the Manchu troops do to my province, I wasn't going to give them one bit of cash.

"Of course not." Boots offered the tobacco to Tiny next, but he also shook his head. "But the men from the Fragrant Mountain district are still trying to collect it for the Manchus. There have been battles up and down the province."

Carp also refused the tobacco. "They'll change their minds."

Boots spat out the old lump of tobacco. "There's a lot of face at stake now, boy." He began to worry another bite from the plug.

In the meantime, though, I'd been watching the battle. There seemed to be one fellow who was running around between the two groups and trying to dodge stones. Every now and then I could see him wave his hands and shout urgently, as if he were trying to get them to stop.

I pointed toward him. "That man is crazy. He's going to get his head cracked by a rock."

Tiny shaded his eyes and frowned. "I know that man," he said, as Boots turned around, startled to hear Tiny speak. "He's Foxfire."

Chapter Twenty

I was shocked to see Tiny climb down from the wagon. "Where are you going?" I asked.

"To help Foxfire. He's a friend." That fact seemed enough of a reason for Tiny to walk straight into a massacre like that. I could only shake my head at the immense, quiet strength of my friend.

Carp gripped the wagon as if nothing would make him let go. "You're crazy."

With a sigh, I got up. After all, Foxfire was Cassia's brother. It was getting to be a habit rescuing their family. And I couldn't let Tiny walk into that mess alone. "Well, I'm even crazier."

The driver was staring after Tiny as he marched purposefully toward the town. "I didn't know your friend could talk. Is he a Stranger?"

"It's a long story, and I haven't got the time." I jumped down from the wagon. I was determined not to go back to my old cowardly ways.

"Well, who's your next of kin?" the driver asked. "I want to know where to send your effects."

I looked over my shoulder at him to tell him that his joke was in bad taste, but he seemed perfectly serious. "Send them to Cassia in Three Willows. She'll know what to do with them."

I had to run to catch up with Tiny, who was striding along on those long legs of his.

Tiny barely glanced at me as he kept his worried face turned toward the town. "This isn't your fight."

"I've had my fill of stupidity too." I'm afraid I was puffing a little from the run. "Just tell me why Foxfire might risk his skull like this."

Tiny wound his queue around his neck so that it wouldn't get in his way during a fight. "Half of his letters are about trying to get our people to unite. He's probably trying to make peace. You talked about the same thing on the boat."

I watched Foxfire dodge another barrage of stones. Some of them looked pretty big, and they had been thrown pretty hard; and yet he didn't show any sign of giving up. "But you didn't catch me becoming a human target."

Tiny started to breathe more heavily as the path sloped upward to the town. "Well," he grunted, "there are ordinary dreamers like you and me who have our feet on the ground. And then there are a few dreamers like Foxfire who stay up in the clouds all the time."

The two groups hadn't shown any sign of growing any calmer in the meantime. Underneath their coatings of sweat and dirt, their faces showed red from all the shouting and stone throwing; and their voices were hoarse as if they'd been yelling a long time.

"We're going to cut off your heads tomorrow and throw them into the nearest ditch," shouted one side. And there were enough bruises and cuts on various faces to let me know that some stones had found their marks.

"Come on and try it now," taunted the other.

And all the time Foxfire was urging, "Wait. Wait. We're people of the T'ang. We can be real folk with our own country. But we've got to think beyond family and clan and Fragrant Mountain or Four Districts." Now that I was closer, I could see that he was about medium height, with the same narrow face as Cassia; but he was slightly younger and had a wilder look to his eyes.

"What a family," I muttered. "Both the brother *and* the sister ought to paint targets on their backs."

"Why?" Tiny paused on the edge of town. "They already know how to get into trouble. They just look for the nearest mob and head right for the center." He motioned for me to turn around. "I think that we'd better go in back to back. Could you walk in step with me?"

But now that we were here, I couldn't see what good that would do except to provide two more targets for stones. "This really is crazy." I was beginning to resent Foxfire a little for letting him draw us both into this mess.

"I know it is." Tiny pulled his hat down farther on his head, as if the felt would protect his skull magically. "You could even call it hopeless."

And suddenly I had it. The problem was that we weren't crazy enough. There were all sorts of ways of serving the Light. It wasn't just fighting. It was doing what we did best, so that meant that there was a time for joking as well as for being serious. "Look, we can't match them with force; and Foxfire's made it obvious that we can't match them with words. We need something to distract them."

"I don't have a thunderstorm in my basket." Tiny started forward, but I caught his arm.

"Laughter distracts even better than fear." I handed him my hat and started to strip off my shirt.

"What are you doing?" Tiny was more alarmed at my odd behavior than by the mob.

When I jerked off my shirt, I could see his face again. "My act."

"What?" Tiny drew his eyebrows together as I pulled off my boots.

"Everyone loves a clown." I pulled up my pants legs.

"Unless he's a bad clown," Tiny warned.

"Well, at least they'll have a new target besides Foxfire." After all Cassia's efforts to make me be more serious, it would be ironical if my clowning saved her brother. I'd have to tell that to her in the first letter I dictated—though that letter was getting to be the size of a book.

Taking a deep breath, I gave a high, piercing whoop. Some of the men nearby turned to look at me, but not everyone heard. But at least it was a start at making my own audience. I said a little prayer to

Ducky and the Gallant to help me wherever they were. And then I gave a kick into the air.

The world seemed to spin by as I turned upside down. I felt the dirt on my palms and the hardness of a pebble and then my legs were swinging down again and I was moving upright past the startled faces. Even Foxfire had stopped dead in his tracks to stare. A stone whizzed by, and I almost fell over; but somehow I managed to go on. At least the others seemed to see me in time, because I didn't see or hear any more.

"Help me, Ducky," I muttered. I swung my feet down one last time and planted them in the dirt; and though I staggered a little, for once I didn't fall down. I spread my arms in triumph. "Gentlemen," I announced in rolling tones, "thank you for assembling. I want to present, direct from Canton and Peking, for your delight and edification, a pageant of skill and martial prowess."

I looked at a man in his sixties. Though he wore the robe and vest of a merchant, he had a stone in his hand. "Sir, would you toss that little pebble to me?"

He seemed surprised and almost shocked that I was talking to him. "Are you addressing me?" He spoke in the Middle Mountain dialect.

"Yes, you." I held out my palm. "If you'd be so kind."

He hesitated, looking around at the others, but none of them seemed sure what to do. No one ever knows what to do with someone who's crazy. However, he must have decided to humor me, because he finally pitched the rock underhanded to me. It arced high in the air.

Ducky and I had practiced with hard-boiled eggs sometimes, or balls made of dried clay. I'm afraid a rock—and a heavy one at that—was another proposition. I had wanted to catch it and fling it into the air so I could begin to juggle, but it hurt my palm and I dropped it. "Whoops." It landed near my foot and I pretended to hop as if it had actually struck my toe. It had always gotten laughs back in my village, but the audiences in Eden were tougher. I didn't hear one laugh.

So I pretended to limp around. "That wasn't the right stone." I turned to a man with a mustache thin as a string. "You, sir. May I try your stone?"

He didn't even hesitate as he flung the stone underhanded to me. This time, I caught it in both hands and pretended to stagger around. Suddenly I stopped dead as if the weight were too much and slowly tilted backward until I fell down. It wasn't the best idea, since I fell on assorted rocks that had reached the ground during the argument. There were a few chuckles at that.

Encouraged, I sat up and grabbed a few small rocks and jumped to my feet before I began to juggle. The stones flipped around my head in a circle, though I wasn't sure how long I could keep that up. I tried to remember as much as I could of Ducky's act. "It's only the beginning, folks. Only the beginning. You will see feats of physical skill that have astounded audiences all over the Middle Kingdom." A man even gave a cheer, and I couldn't help thinking that they really must be starved for entertainment up here. "But first, my assistant will pass among you. We need help to reach the next camp, gentlemen." And I glanced at Tiny. "Tiny, if you'd be so kind."

Tiny picked up on his cue perfectly and, sweeping off his hat, held the brim in both hands as he began to move through the crowd. Foxfire turned and his mouth dropped open as if he couldn't quite believe his eyes when he saw Tiny. There hadn't been any way to warn him in advance, because we would have arrived at the same time as the letter informing him of our trip. At any rate, he didn't say anything as Tiny went on wriggling his hat at the nearest men.

The crowd either ignored him or, more importantly, began to move away in ones and twos. As Ducky had once told me, the easiest trick to perform is to make an audience disappear, and the fastest way to do that is to ask them for money.

Whenever I dropped the stones, I would pick them up and start over again as if I wasn't going to budge from the street. We were winning—people were drifting away—when a voice demanded, "Where are you going? We're not finished yet. We've got to drive these fools from the mountains."

I turned to see that same hunched figure that I could never forget now. It was Dusty. He must have fled over here like so many others after the failure of the rebellion. He was urging on the man in the merchant robe now. I headed straight for him. I would have liked nothing better than to have bounced a stone off his head, but I was here to stop a riot, not start one. I forced myself to smile. "After the show, though."

Dusty glared at me. "It'll be hard to juggle without any arms."

"Then how about having us as a warm-up." I managed to drop two stones so that I was simply palming one.

Dusty would have started for me, but the merchant stopped him. "We don't have any quarrel with that fool."

Dusty leaned his head to one side as if he almost recognized me but could not quite. "Don't I know you from somewhere?"

I stooped quickly, though I doubt if he could remember a single boy from one village. "If you've been to the court of the emperor, perhaps—"

"Carp," the old man said in surprise.

Carp moved past us to the old man. "I finally made it, Father, but it wasn't easy." He glanced over his shoulder at me and then looked back at his father. "What's been happening?"

The old man raised his arms over his head. "What hasn't been happening?"

"How about telling me over tea," Carp suggested.

"Of course. You must be parched from your trip." The old man patted Carp on the back, and they made their own way toward one of the buildings that seemed to be some kind of store. The other Fragrant Mountain men began to drift away, but Dusty stayed long enough to point at me. "You were lucky today, boy." Then he strode off after the old man.

At the same time the other group has also begun to dribble away like a clod of dirt dissolving in water. I'd never known it could feel so good to drive an audience away. Finally there were only Foxfire, Tiny, and myself in the street—and a lot of stones.

"Tiny!" Foxfire said and spread his arms.

"Up to the same old tricks, I see." Tiny threw his arms around Foxfire and gave him a big hug. "Your sister sends her regards."

But almost immediately, Foxfire winced and pushed him away. "Careful. I've got bruises from head to toe." He turned to look at me again. "It's strange, but I have the feeling that I know you."

It felt odd to confront the young man whose footsteps I'd been following all this time. Perhaps he had been with Cassia on the morning of that raid, but I didn't think I ought to remind him of that. "I've got a letter of introduction from your sister."

Tiny waved a hand at me. "He fought with your father and sister at Canton."

I threw the last stone away. "So take that into account when you hear that I'm from Phoenix Village."

It took several breaths for that to register. "What?"

I held up an index finger. "Now remember your own speech. We have to think beyond petty feuds. We're all children of the T'ang."

But Foxfire not only looked like his sister, he also had that same reckless stubbornness. "Your clan nearly took our heads off one morning." He began to ball his hands into fists.

It didn't seem like the time to point out to him that his sister had done her best to take off mine a second time. It looked like the unity and harmony of the T'ang people was going to end right there with a fistfight in the middle of the street. However, Tiny quickly came to my rescue.

Grabbing Foxfire by his collar, Tiny hoisted him off the street so that Foxfire's feet were kicking in the air. "Hear what he has to say first."

Foxfire glared at Tiny. "I thought you were on my side."

Tiny gave Foxfire a little shake that made his teeth clack together. "I'm on *both* your sides. He turned his back on his clan to help me and your sister."

Foxfire just hung there like a limp bag of rice. "He did?"

"He's risked a lot for me and your family." Tiny set Foxfire down on his feet. "Shame on you. You're the last one I expected to attack him. He came to help you, you know."

"That's right." Despite everything, I was beginning to like Foxfire. He might be a big man among the guests and he might be a magician at finding gold, but he still had the same single-mindedness that his sister had. Assuming that I survived this first meeting, he would be easy to tease. In the meantime, though,

I tried to remember some of the things that Cassia had recited from memory. "What about all that talk about putting aside past differences to build a new person?"

Foxfire unclenched his fists. "You do know my letters to my sister."

I wagged a finger at him. "And she wouldn't like it if you tried to rearrange my face."

Foxfire winced as he straightened his shirt—as if he could just picture Cassia. "No, I don't suppose she would." He glanced toward the men around the store who had been watching the whole spectacle. "Let's go to my cabin. We can talk in private up there." Wheeling around, he motioned for us to follow him.

Chapter Twenty-One

We walked up a hill away from the town into a small hollow. After the hot, dusty trip, my body almost seemed to drink up the cool shade. Tall, conelike trees and giant, mistlike ferns rose on either side of us as we walked over the thick carpet of needlelike leaves. There was enough fuel and mulch on the valley floor to have kept a family for a year. Ahead of us, hidden by the trees, was the sound of water.

Now that we were safe from eavesdroppers, Foxfire nudged Tiny. "Now tell me what you're doing here."

Tiny spoke the words painfully—as if they were

being pulled one by one from him. "Aster's dead."

Foxfire looked shocked. "No. How?"

"I'm trying to think of it as another country and long ago." The big man seemed to have sunk deep within himself as if he were fighting his own private demons. "It's probably all in your sister's letter."

I slipped the letter from my bundle. "Your early letters were dictated to other writers. Can you get someone to read it to you?"

"I learned how to read and write a little." Foxfire took it from me and gave me a suspicious look. "But how do you know that I used to have others write for me?"

I used the brim of my hat to wipe some of the sweat from my forehead.

I looked over my shoulder at him. "I told you. I know your sister. She might have written about me in the letter too."

Foxfire tore the envelope and slipped the letter out. "I just can't figure what she's doing reading my private letters to a Phoenix." He caught my arm. "Look out."

I turned and saw a small stream I'd almost fallen into. "Thanks," I said to Foxfire.

Foxfire motioned to the right. "Just follow the stream." And he began to read the letter.

We walked slowly, because Foxfire had to read the letter. Somehow Foxfire's hollow seemed the last place to be reading about feuds and wars. Where the stream dashed past the rocks, it formed a white froth; but where it flowed free it was a dark, jadelike green.

Farther on I could see the calmer, deeper parts, where the water was so still and deep, it almost seemed as if I were looking through a special piece of glass instead of at the rocks and fish. Then a twig fell into the water, creating ripples that spread in small circles, and the rock and the fish seemed to shimmer and lose their shape.

When he was finished, Foxfire refolded his sister's letter. "Well," he admitted to me, "you must be all right if Cassia trusts you. She doesn't take to many people." But he seemed even more puzzled than before.

But Tiny formed an impenetrable wall. "He's all right, I tell you. We've been through a lot together."

Foxfire hesitated as if he weren't so sure about Tiny's judgment, but after a moment he simply raised one shoulder. "Well, I'm sorry about Aster."

Tiny forcibly pulled up the corners of his mouth. "I still have a son. There's a world to build for him; one without these stupid wars."

I ran a hand through my hair and snatched it back

when I felt the needle that was still in my queue. "Like the war we walked into."

Foxfire slipped the letter back into the envelope. "And the next week it could be two other groups."

"But this war sounds serious. I saw Dusty." I wondered that he hadn't done anything about him. As the old saying goes, a son shouldn't sleep under the same sky as his father's murderer. "You know about your father?"

"Yes, Cassia wrote me." He walked with great care, as if he had to concentrate on putting one foot in front of the other. "But if I've learned one thing here, it's that we have to forget about our own personal hates."

Even if I didn't accept his thinking, he was being consistent with what he'd written in his letters. I couldn't be sure what that cost him, though, so I tried to change the subject. "What's Dusty doing collecting a tax for the Manchus?" I sucked the drop of blood that welled up on my thumb.

Foxfire jammed his sister's letter up his sleeve. "Leave it to Dusty. He's like a vulture who knows where to find misery. He's only interested in whoever will pay him. I think he's the one who talked the Barber into setting up a battle for tomorrow."

"Was the Barber that old fellow in the robe?" My free hand played with the crown of my hat.

"Yes." Foxfire skipped over a small gully. "They call him the Barber because he shaves his customers so close when they come to his store."

"Shaves?" I rubbed my own chin.

"He's a good bargainer." Foxfire balanced on a root. "But I think he made a bad bargain when he hired Dusty. Up to now the fighting in Eden has been with words and fists. Once blood is shed . . ." Foxfire's voice trailed off and he just shook his head.

I thought I understood. "Then the feuding will start here just like at home."

Foxfire used the brim of his battered felt hat to wipe the sweat from his forehead. "It gets worse than that. Some *Americans* are already complaining about the battles that have been fought so far. They'd like to use them as an excuse to ship us all home. This just gives them more ammunition."

I rested an arm over my stomach. More and more I felt as if I had jumped out of a whirlpool and into a hole that was about to collapse on me at any moment. And at the same time I was beginning to understand just why Foxfire had held back from his own personal revenge. "But the authorities can't want warfare in their state."

Holding the crown of his hat, Foxfire set it back on top of his head. "It depends. In some places they've kept them from fighting; but up here the *sheriff* would just as soon see us kill one another."

"Wait," I said excitedly. "We saved the Barber's son. He owes us a favor. Maybe we could get him to talk some sense to his father."

Foxfire adjusted the brim of his hat. "That's impossible. You'd get your head shot off if you came within three meters of that store."

There was a branch overhanging the trail by the stream. I put a hand to it and swung it back. "That's mighty hard on the Barber's customers, isn't it?"

Foxfire stepped past me. "That's just on the eve of battle."

Tiny followed Foxfire. "I could go. They'd know from my accent that I'm a Stranger and not likely to side with men from the Three *or* Four Districts. And Carp knows me."

I swung the branch over the trail. "You've got a boy. It's better if I go."

Tiny pointed out, "The guards would be suspicious of your accent."

Foxfire snapped the brim of his hat down with a quick flick of his wrists. "Neither one of you is going. I'm the one for the job."

Tiny shook his head. "Carp would never leave to talk with you."

Foxfire smiled ruefully. "Cassia told—no, she ordered me to watch out for you two and see that you got settled. I don't cross my sister often."

He might be an important man over here, but he still was Cassia's little brother. I suppose we all have our weak points with relatives. I had Uncle Itchy. He had Cassia. "She believes in dying for causes," I said. "What could be a better cause than peace? But if you're still worried about your sister, I'll dictate a letter explaining everything to her."

Annoyed, Foxfire paused in mid step. "I don't need protection from my own sister."

I shifted my bundle to my other arm. "Well, don't make her sound like an ogre either."

Foxfire turned sideways so he could look at me as he began to walk again. "What's Cassia to you, anyway?"

I hesitated, unsure of what to say to the man who might be my brother-in-law. "A friend." I added, "A special one."

"How special?" Foxfire demanded.

"I think that I've said enough." I got ready to drop my bundle and fight if I had to. I hadn't come all this way to put myself under another bully like Lumpy.

My words just seemed to irritate Foxfire more. He jabbed a finger at me. "Listen, Phoenix. Don't you come onto my claim and start telling me what to do."

Tiny stepped between us. "Don't be jealous just because Cassia's found someone."

Foxfire tapped his fingers against his chest. "I'm not jealous."

"Well, you're giving a good imitation of it." Taking Foxfire's shoulders, Tiny forcibly turned his friend forward again.

As the big man pushed him along, Foxfire protested, "But he's a Phoenix."

Tiny's arms stiffened as if he were having to use all of his strength to keep Foxfire going. "He's all right, I tell you. Cassia's chosen well."

Foxfire looked over his shoulder angrily. "I'm the head of the family now that Father's dead."

Tiny simply chuckled. "First of all, I think Cassia would be surprised to hear that. Secondly, you're over here and she's back home. Either way you don't have much say in what she does."

Foxfire thought that over and then sighed reluctantly. "No, I guess not."

"So I'll go get Carp," I insisted again. "My uncle Itchy says that I can talk my way into anything. Armed guards won't stop me.

I could see that I had crawled up a notch in Foxfire's estimation. "You'd be willing to risk it?"

I brushed some hair from my forehead back underneath my hat. "I didn't know your father long before he died, but he said a few things to me that went deep. He talked about bringing out the Light in everyone."

Foxfire laughed wearily—as if that had been an old argument with his father. "The Light is just another name for an old dynasty. It belongs on the trash heap with a lot of other outmoded notions."

I remembered what Cassia had told me about his letters. I suppose he preferred an *American*-style government. "But you can't have a government of equal people. It's like having everyone be king. Everyone would be giving orders." I slapped a hand against my leg for emphasis. "It'd be chaos."

"No, no." Foxfire's face had taken on that dreamy, excited look. "The best person usually comes to the job—just like the best usually comes out in a person, too."

"What do you mean?" Tiny wondered.

"It'll be easier to show you." Suddenly the trees gave way and we were clambering over a huge mound of gravel and waste. "Come on." In his eagerness to show us the truth, he'd become just like a little boy as he jumped nimbly onto a boulder and then behind it.

Tiny and I, being more ordinary sort of plodders, both had to hurry up to keep up with Foxfire. When we rounded the pile of rubble, we found ourselves facing the oddest contraption. It was a series of troughs, one connected into the other—looking like a coffin for a giant snake. They began in the middle of a field by a huge hole, and angled down the bank of the stream to the water's edge.

Water was carried from the stream to the middle of the field by a rattling water chain like at home. The water chain consisted of a series of boards mounted on a moving belt in a large trough. A man worked the foot pedals to keep the belt moving. The water would then sweep down a wooden duct to the troughs.

Tiny slowed and patted the side of the trough. "What's this for?"

Foxfire picked up a shovel that had been leaning against the trough. "This is how we find gold." Impatient to make a point, he used his booted foot to jab the shovel deep into the dirt. "Just because you can't see the golden mountain doesn't mean it isn't there." Almost feverishly, he lifted the shovel of dirt up and dumped it into a screen set at the top of the trough just a few feet from the end of the water chain.

With quick, strong twists of his wrist, he deftly flicked the large rocks and pebbles out of the screen.

Even when the water chain was not running, there was always a little water in the trough, and that water was clouded now as if there were some shining milky-brown cloth dropped inside the length of the troughs.

Throwing down the shovel, Foxfire darted over to the foot pedals of the water chain. Soon I heard the familiar creak of the treadle board and the rattling of the wooden chain within its own special trough, but the eager Foxfire was working it at a pace that I'd never seen before. Water was swept spasmodically from the stream into the first trough. The water level began to rise in one trough after another until it splashed out of the lower end onto the stream bank again.

"Gold's heavier than the dirt," Foxfire panted to us, "so it settles out along the cleats on the bottom of the trough.

Under the pressure of the water flowing downward, the dirt and pebbles moved restlessly over the cleats—swept along as if by some invisible hand. The sunlight shone in folds and wrinkles on the surface of the water, but suddenly there was an answering flash of light from deep within the trough—almost as if there were an infant sun being born inside there.

"I think I see something," Tiny called.

Foxfire jumped down and raced over to us. "The best always appears—whether it's in dirt or among people." And he plunged his hand into the trough, searching about the mud gathered by the cleats. Finally he lifted his fist triumphantly into the air. "It's like the truth." Slowly, he unfolded his dripping fingers to reveal a tiny flake of gold. "We have so much to learn from the Westerners." He was careful to use another name that I had heard for *Americans*.

From the eager expression on his face, you would have thought he'd found a nugget the size of a fist. It was the same look that his father had worn when he was talking about the Light and that his sister had worn speaking about the Work. His whole family was a wild set of dreamers—each in his or her way.

If he was anything like his sister, he would be ready to elaborate his point for the rest of the day. "Listen, you can lecture me some other time about demon governments, manners, or hairstyles. Right now, we have more immediate problems—like heading off a bloodbath."

His damp fingers closed round the flake. "Oh, that's right." He looked a little disappointed, though, that his fancy couldn't go on soaring among the clouds.

I leaned against the trough. "So what do I have to say to convince you two that I'm the one to get Carp?"

"No, I'm the one to get Carp," Tiny rumbled in his deep voice.

"Think of your son," I warned.

Tiny turned to me, and he looked almost as serious as Cassia could. "I am thinking of Otter. It's time to spread some of that light you were talking about."

"I'm no coward now," I insisted to Tiny.

"I know, but neither am I." Tiny nodded to Foxfire. "You know that I'm the best person for the job."

Foxfire scratched behind his ear unhappily. "I know, but it's so risky."

Tiny closed his hand around Foxfire's shoulder as if that could make Foxfire understand better. "All my life I've been quiet and minded my own business so the stupid people would ignore me. Only I found out that they don't. And doing nothing only lets the stupidity spread. It's time to fight this kind of stupidity wherever we find it."

Foxfire looked at me. "He's right, you know."

"Well, now—" I said unhappily.

"You've been outvoted," Tiny declared firmly.

Chapter Twenty-Two

We decided that Foxfire and I would wait outside town among the trees while Tiny went to get Carp. "So you liked my father." Foxfire studied me as if that made me a curiosity.

I leaned against a tree. "I was sorry when he died."

Bracing his legs against the ground, he set his back against a tree as if he had to hold it up all by himself. "She wrote me when it happened." He added thoughtfully, "But she didn't mention you."

I thought that was an interesting choice that Cassia

had made. "Your father kept your sister from killing me."

He cocked his head to the side curiously. "Relations seemed to have improved since then."

"Your sister can be quite pleasant if you can survive the first meeting."

Foxfire frowned skeptically. "Cassia?"

I folded my arms. "Your sister has a lot of good qualities."

He scratched behind his neck. "Oh, I know that. It's just that there were so many bad ones that go along with them."

I gave a laugh. "What do brothers know?"

He glanced at me shrewdly. "What do boyfriends know?"

I slowly squatted, sliding my back down the tree. "Seeing as how we're almost related, why don't you tell me how you get gold from worthless claims."

He kicked at a pinecone. "It won't work if too many people do it."

I wrapped my arms around my knees. "I don't know what's in her letter to you, but your sister probably asked you to help Tiny and me."

"So?"

I voiced the plan that I'd figured out on our way up to Eden. "Well, hire us to work for you; and when you leave for the Middle Kingdom, we can start practicing your secret for ourselves."

He shot a warning look at me. "Easy, Phoenix. Don't plan my future for me."

But I was beginning to have my fill of the mighty Foxfire. "Never mind," I snapped. "I don't want your charity. Tiny and I can always find work elsewhere."

He drew his head back quizzically, as if that new angle could help him understand me. "You're serious."

I put on my best Cassia look. "Very."

He sighed reluctantly. "I do want to go home sometime."

I did my best to hide my triumphant smile. "Then it looks like you've just hired two workers."

He looked all around as if secrecy were almost instinctive now. "Well, you know that they get the gold dust from the water. It had to be dried out at night."

"So?" I raised an eyebrow at him.

"I noticed that no matter how careful someone is, some of the dust blows away as it dries."

I scratched my head. "And the miners didn't try and get it?"

"It was only a little bit—not enough to make it worthwhile trying to reclaim." He added smugly,

"But over the weeks and months and even years that 'little bit' of dust begins to accumulate."

I suddenly got to my feet as I realized how simple and how brilliant his secret was. "And it accumulates and accumulates until it is worthwhile to go through the dirt from the cabin floor."

He pointed a finger at me. "That's right. I actually work the dirt from the cabin floor. After months and even years, the dirt can be pretty rich."

"You only pretend to work the field."

"Until I've finished with the cabin floor," he explained. "Then I go on to a new 'worthless' claim."

I clapped my right hand over my left fist and dipped my head. "I bow to a true master."

He wriggled his shoulders. "You know, I feel better after having told someone."

I spread my hands. "Well, now you can take it easy and let us pretend to do the work."

He slipped his hands behind his head. "And spend some time on the real business at hand: learning what we can from the Westerners."

I held up a hand as I saw a lantern bobbing toward us. It was Tiny and Carp. Carp grimaced when he saw me. "I figured you were behind all this. My father nearly had a heart attack when I told him I was going out."

I dusted off my trousers. "Sorry, but we figured you were the only one who could stop that nonsense tomorrow."

Carp's head reared back. "My father promised to pay the assessment that the Manchus want from the miners to put down the rebellions back home."

"Then let him pay it," Foxfire said. "He can always collect it later from his customers. There's no one quite like the Barber at shaving the folk who come into his store."

I jerked my head at Carp. "What if we had gone by the old prejudices? You might not be here."

Carp ran an unhappy hand underneath his queue. "I know, I know."

"We've got enough to worry about from the *Americans*," Foxfire argued, "without having to worry about one another."

"Now is the time to show a united front," I added.

Carp flung up his hand impatiently. "All right, all right. I'll do what I can."

"Well, isn't that sweet." Dusty stepped out from behind a tree. In his hand he had a large demon handgun. "Your father thought you might be in danger, so he sent me along. Little did he know."

Carp regarded him coldly. Apparently he didn't lose any more love for Dusty than we did. "I'm perfectly safe, as you can see, so you can go back."

Dusty strode forward, the barrel of his gun resting against his shoulder. "I hardly call it safe when the son of a dangerous rebel lures you out here." He grinned as Foxfire gave a start. "Oh, yes, I know who you are. I've been waiting to pay your father back."

"That is another quarrel for another place," Foxfire insisted. He dropped his hands to his sides as if he were getting ready to rush him.

Dusty lifted up the gun and caressed the barrel with his free hand. He was like a child delighting in a new toy. "But it is my quarrel when you try and stop my livelihood."

I copied Foxfire, tensing for a leap at Dusty. "There'll still be plenty of fighting for you somewhere else."

Dusty took a step backward so he could keep an eye on both of us. "Your family isn't nearly so big when someone else has a gun. And I'll warn you: This gun has six shots, not two like your father's."

"Go back to the store," Carp ordered. "These are my friends."

Dusty cradled the gun between both his palms. "You only think that they're your friends. But they only want to lure you out here to kill you like the treacherous dogs they are."

Foxfire started to charge toward Dusty, but Dusty quickly gripped the gun once again in his right hand and aimed it at Foxfire.

Foxfire froze, staring at the barrel. His shoulders sagged as if he knew the game was lost already. "And you'll come along and avenge him."

Carp gave Dusty a bewildered look. "Whatever for?"

Dusty thumbed back the hammer. "I can probably talk that old fool into paying a bounty for avenging his beloved son."

"And if you play your cards right," Foxfire said thoughtfully, "you can fan the fight into a full-scale war."

Dusty nodded his head. "There's money to be made for a smart man."

"But my father hired you," Carp said, outraged. "That makes you our employee."

"It's hard to find good help nowadays," Foxfire said.

It was now or never, I told myself. He was going to shoot me anyway, but perhaps I could give the others the time to stop him. I took a step forward and my foot cracked some twig. Dusty swung around to aim his gun at me. And it was strange to know that I was going to die—almost quieting. It was going to be up to the others now.

"Dusty," Tiny shouted, and crashed through the brush toward him.

Dusty whirled around and fired. The impact of the lead ball halted Tiny in his tracks. Dusty seemed almost puzzled, though, that Tiny was still standing. He fired again, and though Tiny's body shook from the second lead ball, he still remained standing there. With an anguished cry, Foxfire flung himself at Dusty. I leaped at the man a moment later.

But Tiny was closer. Like some solid, heavy tree, he literally fell against Dusty, and his big hands closed around Dusty's wrists. "I'm tired of your kind," Tiny shouted. And the two toppled backward.

I picked up a rock. "Tiny, roll on your side," I ordered.

But Tiny simply remained above Dusty as if his one purpose in life now was to hold the man pinned to the ground. Both their faces strained; and though I couldn't see what they were doing, I figured that Dusty was probably trying to aim the gun at Tiny.

I was still trying to think of some way to help Tiny

when I thought I heard bones crunch and Dusty gave an agonized scream, and I remembered that Tiny had once been a blacksmith. There was probably still a blacksmith's strength in his hands and arms.

"No, no." Dusty's head was twisting from side to side in pain. Suddenly the gun exploded. Tiny's head shot up in surprise, and Dusty grew still.

"Tiny." Dropping the rock, I pulled at his shoulders and Tiny slid away from Dusty.

Dusty was lying there with the gun in his left hand now. He lifted his head just enough to look at the bloody wound in his stomach. Tiny had managed to twist his hand so that Dusty had shot himself. Then Dusty looked first at Foxfire and then at me. "It's not going to end here. Not for any of you." He made it sound like a curse. He struggled to raise the gun in his left hand, but the barrel shook uncontrollably.

"He can't even die well." A disgusted Foxfire kicked the gun from his hands. It crashed into the nearby bushes.

As if the gun were the last thing holding him to the earth, Dusty gave a sigh and sagged to the ground, dead.

"Get help," I ordered Carp, and knelt beside Tiny. He was swaying back and forth on his knees. He was a strong man, terribly strong, but even with all his strength, he couldn't hold on to life. "You'll take care of my son?" he asked me.

"As if he were my own," I promised.

He smiled slowly. "Aster and I will do what we can."

"Hold on, Tiny." My voice almost broke with anger at him for giving up. "We didn't come all this way to end like this."

But his eyes closed and he fell backward.

Foxfire straightened out Tiny's legs. "There's no way he could have survived those wounds."

Intending to straighten out his arms, I pried open the fingers of one fist. The little gold flake fell to the dirt. I picked it up and held it out to Foxfire on the ball of my finger. "This wasn't so lucky."

"Gold rarely is," Foxfire said.

Chapter Twenty-Three

As soon as he had heard the shots, the Barber had come running with a dozen armed men. He was pretty shaken up when he saw his mercenary, Dusty, dead on the ground, and even more shaken up when Carp told him what his mercenary had tried to do.

The Barber looked at the gun in his own hand as if it were about to explode at any moment. "He made it sound like it was so important to drive rebels out of the gold fields. He kept telling us how *American* gold was going to pay for chaos at home."

I looked over at the dead Dusty. "I bet he got the guns for you, didn't he?"

The Barber handed the gun to a man behind him. "He said he knew where he could get a lot of them."

"And make a profit." I brushed some dirt from Tiny's face.

"That's all he was interested in." Carp took his father's arm. "He didn't care how many men died."

"Call a truce before there are any more senseless deaths," Foxfire urged. "We've got enough troubles in the gold fields without making more for ourselves."

The Barber shook his head. "But I've summoned all those men. I'll lose face."

"Peacemakers never lose face." I folded Tiny's arms over his stomach. "Call a truce."

Carp might have been a nuisance during the trip here, but he had his good points after all. He gave his father's arm a little shake now. "Then everyone will know that you're magnanimous as well as cunning."

"Or will they call it weakness?" the Barber wondered.

I rose and pointed at Tiny. "Then you write the letter to this man's son. He's already lost his mother. Now his father's gone as well." I jerked my head at him. "And you write letters to all the wives and mothers and fathers and children who lose someone to-morrow."

The Barber stared down at Tiny's corpse. "You shouldn't put all the blame on me. The others wanted war too."

"But you can stop it," Carp coaxed.

The Barber looked from his son to us and back again. It was as if he were afraid of losing his son's respect. Suddenly he thrust out a hand toward us. "I'm a man of business, not of war. What am I trying to do?"

"You'll call the truce?" Foxfire asked.

The Barber nodded. "As they say, 'There's no profit in war.'"

Some of the Barber's men gave us a hand taking Tiny's body back up to the cabin. It was a small, drafty little shack with a bare dirt floor. The place smelled of dust and smoke and mildew; Foxfire had tried to cover the cracks between the wallboards with old newspapers.

I just wish some of the folk back home could have seen how one of the richest men lived. The cabin was short on furniture and long on books and notes. Boxes had been dragged together to form a desktop, on which rested an open demon-style book with pictures and simple words, so I assumed it was a child's primer.

Apparently, Foxfire was trying to learn the demon tongue as well. Next to the primer was a pile of both demon and T'ang books, and close to them was a smoke-blackened lantern and notes painstakingly written on broad sheets of demon paper. I guess that after a hard day's work, Foxfire put in additional hours studying.

The Barber had also sent up one of the many coffins that had been in anticipation of the battle tomorrow—along with a promise that we could have help tomorrow burying our friend. It was too hard shipping an entire body back home, so the custom was to wait a number of years and then ship the bones back for final burial.

When everyone was gone, Foxfire made us some tea. "I don't know what I'm going to tell Cassia," Foxfire worried. "I was supposed to look out for you."

I began to sort through Tiny's things. The clothes, I guess, could be given to someone; but Tiny's worn wooden Buddha ought to be shipped back for his son to keep. There was a spot of blood on it, and I toyed with the idea of cleaning it off, but decided against it. His son could always do that when he was old enough. In the meantime, I'd make sure that little Otter would never need money. "Carp would never have gone with you. I'm the one who'll be in trouble with her. He might have gone with me."

Foxfire ran a hand over his face. "Then I should have come up with another plan that wouldn't have risked either of your lives."

It was strange to have met the father and now the son. They both tried to take on too much—well, so did the sister, too. I was getting to like him. "I'm not going to argue about who's going to get more blame from Cassia."

He grimaced. "No, I suppose there are more important things to worry about."

I dragged myself over to a chair—feeling as if I were a hundred—and sat down. "We'll just tell her the truth. Tiny knew the risks, but he also knew that there was more at stake than just his life."

Foxfire swung around with a smirk. "You think that will satisfy Cassia?"

I set the little wooden Buddha and its thong on the table alongside the little gold flake. "No," I had to admit, "but she might feel better when you tell her that you put an end to Dusty."

"*We* put an end to Dusty." He set a cup of tea in front of me.

"Well," I sighed, "your poor father's ghost can rest now."

Foxfire stood there for a moment while he studied me. Finally he nodded his head. "You know, you're not bad for a Phoenix."

"And you're not bad for a Young." I kicked out my legs in front of me.

He rubbed his chin. "You might even be all right as a brother-in-law."

I laced my fingers over my belly. "So far I've managed to get out of every scrape your family's gotten me into."

He gave a sad little laugh. "I'm afraid that you haven't seen anything yet."

That was probably true, but that didn't scare me—not so long as the Light stayed with me. "I'm ready." I sipped the tea, and the fragrant aroma seemed to fill my mouth and nose. It was like having the sunset inside my cup. I lowered the cup and looked down at the tea. "This is delicious."

Foxfire took a sip of his own tea. "It comes from bushes in another province back home."

He seemed to take it so matter-of-factly, but I had to hold the cup away from me. The tea had probably come even farther than I had. I found myself wondering if Cassia would have liked it. "It's strange that both the tea and I should come so far to meet over here."

Foxfire swung his leg over the bench and sat down. "But a little bit of everything comes to *America*—including news. I probably know more about what's happening in the Middle Kingdom in general than you do."

I thought for a moment about what it was like to be a guest of the golden mountain and to expect such extraordinary things. Smiley and Boots and now Foxfire all seemed to suggest a different way of life—a life changed by the wild, strange, exciting things that they were learning from the *Americans*. "I feel like one of those people in those tales who wander onto a mountain and meet magical creatures."

Foxfire grinned ruefuly. "One thing's for sure: You'll never be the same."

That sent a strange, lonely chill down my spine; but I shook off that mood after a moment. Would Cassia know me when I got back home?

Foxfire rose abruptly and jerked the door open. "Look outside."

The sky was filled with a soft, red twilight while the trees and ground were bathed in a strange, golden light as if we were all trapped inside a yellow crystal. "Once, back at home when I was small, we had a sunrise like this, and my mother said that it looked like the light was coming from each of us."

I held up my hand. It seemed to be carved from the very light itself. "It does, doesn't it?"

"I only saw it a few times back at home," Foxfire mused. "And it was never as bright as this, and it never happened as often."

I looked at Foxfire, and it was like seeing Cassia's face—only more clearly. I wished she were here to see it as well. "It's a mountain light, then," I said.

Foxfire mulled that notion over for a moment, and then nodded his head thoughtfully. His eyes had taken on that same wildness that I had seen earlier—no, seeing his face in the mountain light let me see that it wasn't a wildness. I'd been wrong about Foxfire the dreamer. Wildness sounded too reckless, and this was an energy that was under control—like the flight of a hawk. He slapped my arm approvingly. "It's a light to spread from here all the way overseas and back home."

I raised my cup to him. "To a mountain light then."

He lifted his cup to me in turn. "And the end of stupidity."

I lowered my cup after drinking. "And what happens afterward? In the tales they also change enough so that they can never really go home."

Foxfire pursed his lips as if he had never anticipated

that part of his future. "I suppose that may happen to us, too."

It was still a little frightening to think about some of the changes that would come. But I almost thought I could hear good old practical Tiny whisper to us from the cabin, "It might be a change for the better though."

"Well," I said as the last of the sunlight bathed our faces, "whatever happens, we'll make the best of it. As your sister would say, we don't have much choice."

Afterword

The events in this novel occur in the period between the spring and fall of 1855. For an account of the Red Turban revolt and the subsequent persecution of the Hakka (the Strangers), see Frederick Wakeman's *Strangers at the Gate*.

The conflicts in the California gold fields between Americans and Chinese and among the Chinese themselves are described in the newspaper accounts of that period. Further reading may be done in H. Mark Lai and Philip P. Choy's *Outlines: A History of the Chinese in America* and in Ruthann Lum McCunn's *An Illustrated History of the Chinese in America*.